P9-AQL-758

DREAMING JUNGLES

A Pantheon Modern Writers Original

Translated from the French
by William R. Carlson

PANTHEON BOOKS NEW YORK

DREAMING

Michel Rio

JUNGLES

The invaluable help of the author and of Margery Safir in the preparation of the English text is gratefully acknowledged.

Translation Copyright © 1987 by Random House, Inc.

Originally published in France as *Les Jungles Pensives* by Editions André Balland. Copyright © 1985 by Éditions Balland.

Library of Congress Cataloging-in-Publication Data
Rio, Michel.
Dreaming jungles.
Translation of: Les jungles pensives.
I. Title.
PQ2678.I563J8613 1986 843'.914 86-22560
ISBN 0-394-55661-5
ISBN 0-394-75035-7 (pbk.)

Book design by Guenet Abraham

Manufactured in the United States of America

First English Language Edition

To Elisabeth Zadora Laczkowska

DREAMING JUNGLES

The first lieutenant came up to me with a broad smile that was like the silent exordium to a friendly conversation. He was so fresh, childlike, and well brought-up, impeccable to the point of provocation in his immaculately white uniform, that one would have thought he had come directly from his mother's arms and parlor, still covered with kisses and blessings, at the dawn of a voyage to the antipodes uniquely designed to spare him the boredom and immorality of idleness. An absurd apparition in that furnace, he provoked incredulity, admiration, and annoyance. Since the beginning of the crossing, having learned that our families were somehow distantly related, he had surrounded me with a rather encumbering solicitude that combined airy camaraderie with traces of deference, deference due no doubt to the mystery bestowed on me by my scientific occupations and to the fact that I was three or four years his senior.

"I hope, sir, you are not suffering too much from the heat."

"I think I shall survive, Lieutenant. Do you happen to know," I added, turning towards the coast that was slowly passing by, "whether there are any sea crocodiles in these parts?"

He seemed speechless, and his radiant smile disappeared. He must have wondered if I was making fun of him, or perhaps he suspected rudeness in a question that immediately put me beyond his personal competence, or, what amounted to the same thing, put me beyond the universally shared competence that authorizes a polite, general, and meaningless exchange between two willing individuals concerning, for example, the weather, or aesthetics, or morality.

"Sea crocodiles, sir?" he repeated cautiously.

"*Crocodylus porosus*, Lieutenant. It is not a naturalist's joke. I saw some off the coast of Sumatra two years ago, near a mangrove swamp identical to this."

He looked at the coast thoughtfully, as if seeking there a response or at least some attitude to adopt. The ship was plowing silently through a calm sea and thick, stagnant air saturated with water whose resistance and density it seemed to have taken on, the two elements mixing together into a homogeneous and torrid soup. Several cable lengths away, the mangrove swamp besieged the sea. A mixture, too, but of earth and water, it advanced from the solid ground to the open sea in parallel ranks of mangrove trees. It was a garden, half submerged in the fresh water of rivers and marshland that regularly blended with the salty flux of the ocean. A natural chaos and a radically primitive uncertainty, it bred adaptable and unspecialized monsters: beasts of earth and water at the same time, hesitant, at the mercy of the tides. It was, at the dawn of the twentieth century, a living relic of the first biological era, the anachronistic manifestation of an unfinished world where the walking fish was still struggling to climb from the water to the earth, clambering up on its fins, as if the destiny of future species depended on this terrible and derisory perseverance, which seemed the sign of a blind instinct of responsibility. But it was probable that the lieutenant saw none of this in all he surveyed with a gaze devoid of emotion, only slightly disconcerted by this business of the crocodiles.

"No, sir, in three years of service on this line I have never seen a crocodile swimming in the sea. It seems so . . . out of place. I would have remembered it."

"Do you think, Lieutenant, that a crocodile venturing out to sea is any more out of place than we are right now in this primeval hell—or paradise, depending on your taste? Do you think that it would be incapable of behaving, in this apparently absurd environment, with a dignity and good humor which we might envy?"

"If those are your thoughts, sir, what have you come to do in this place?"

"My thoughts on the subject are contradictory. The common origin of species and the oddities of evolution are one of the favorite playgrounds of paradox. Which does not necessarily mean that the profession of naturalist is nothing but alternating bursts of laughter and anguished perplexities. But to answer your question, I have come here to study chimpanzees in their own environment, their behavior with respect to ourselves, and to make my modest contribution to the work of Darwin's successors. Others are doing the same for the gorilla or the orangutan. That would tend to prove, despite my first, traveler's impression, that I do not feel us to be strangers to this savagery, which must also be in our genes, to use Mr. Johanson's word. Nevertheless, when I see you I cannot help suspecting—please take this as a compliment—that God himself created you just as you are."

"Precisely what I believe," said the lieutenant, who had found his smile again. "And I don't think of it in the least as a personal matter. As a result, I don't take any pride in it. And even if I were wrong, it seems to me that aboard this ship it would not have the slightest importance. Here, the fact of feeling more or less out of place is a purely superficial affair, a simple matter of temperature or landscape, for the simple reason that the deck beneath our feet is a piece of France, like Paris or Brittany, the only difference being that it is endowed with a certain speed. You can see that our positions are different and I have nothing to worry about since I am not leaving my environment. That said, would you care to have a drink?"

"By all means."

The next day, shortly before noon, the ship anchored at Grand Bassam, and a light port vessel transported me, with my arms and baggage, to the decrepit wharves, partially rebuilt, where a crowd of officials, merchants and planters, servants, clerks, and sailors was milling about. French foremen hustled along native workers and dockers in a marvelously comical patois, a blend of French dialects and words taken from various local languages. Sheds, warehouses, customs offices, and various administrative and military buildings stood nearby, while further on, opulent houses with wide verandas, surrounded by small gardens, were conceitedly set apart from a jumble of shanties, huts, and stores. The buildings were of stone, brick, or wood, and roofed with tile, tinplate, caulked and tarred planks, or simply thatch and palm branches. All of this made up a motley settlement, at once orderly and anarchic, punctuated with thickets and palm trees, remainders of the original vegetation which bore witness to some colonists' nostalgic desire to imitate with scraps of jungle the splendors of a French garden.

A little man, thin and elegant, surrounded by four sturdy blacks and an armed policeman, was waiting for me on the dock. I noticed right away that he was not sweating, as if miraculously spared by the heat and the humidity. Not one drop formed on his high forehead, his shaved temples, or his birdlike neck thrust into the Prussian stiffness of his starched snow-white shirt. There emanated from him, from his eyes above all, an aura of conscientious tenacity, of chilly and methodical intelligence that suggested a kind of tranquil inhumanity, as if his moral being were as impervious to heat as his skin. Here, I said to myself, is the very essence of the kind of man who invades Africa as if he were going for a walk in the Tuileries. His voice was unexpectedly soft, with something melodious and charming about it that took me a bit off guard.

"Allow me to introduce myself. Blanchot, first secretary to the governor. He received your orders from the Ministry and the Museum in the last mail. He was unable to meet you, because the work on the port and the railroad, as well as the problems of pacification, require him to remain in Abidjan, where he is expecting you today. Welcome. I advise you to wear a hat."

I answered this speech with a few vague remarks. I was drenched in sweat, a bit surprised, and feeling sullen. The blacks picked up my baggage and equipment lined up on the deck, and carried them to a kind of cart. This conveyance was harnessed to a dull-eyed old horse that seemed to be awaiting imminent death with truly stoical patience.

We crossed the city heading north, in the direction of the Ebrié lagoon, making our way with difficulty through a dense crowd, noisy but unexcited, bustling without hurry. The policeman and the porters opened up the way. Blanchot and I walked behind the cart, which the poor nag pulled at a rate suggesting that each step required an effort of will and imagination.

"It is a mosaic, a veritable human mosaic," he said in his pleasant voice. "Here you have mostly Kwa lagoon-dwellers: the Ebrié, Essouma, Avikam, Zéma, Alladian, Eotilé, and Abouré, from the littoral; and, from the interior, the Abidji, Attié, and Abé. Further on, you find the Guéré and Krou from the southwest, the Baoulé and Agni from the open forest, and, from the western mountains, the Dan, Toura, and Wobé. In the north you have savannah dwellers, the Malinké, Sénoufo, Koulango, Lobi, and others I am doubtless forgetting or don't know about. You have fishermen, gatherers, herdsmen, hunters, growers. Peaceful ones and warlike ones. Friendly and hostile. An infinite variety of mentalities and customs. Dozens of languages and dialects. I speak eighteen of them, and that is far from all."

"Eighteen? But how long have you been here?"

"I arrived twenty years ago, in 1893, when this territory became a colony and Binger was appointed the first governor. I started out as a lowly bureaucrat, a kind of undersecretary. I was twenty-four years old. It quickly became obvious to me that neither force, good will, enterprise, rapacity, nor humanitarianism was enough. Too many misunderstandings. A friendly gesture here becomes, just a few miles away, a hostile one. And you find yourself with a piece of wood planted between your shoulder blades, as good a way as any to end the confusion. Then there are reprisals. Too much time and energy, too many people lost. So I started to learn about the country. I took part in the explorations led by Arago, Segonzac, Marchand, Clozel, Monteil, Monnier, Quiquerez, and Tavernost into the interior. I made myself indispensable. A kind of anthropologist or interpreter or peacemaker, depending on the circumstances. I was given more and more responsibility during the period of 'peaceful penetration.' I was nearly appointed governor. My role has somewhat diminished since 1908, when Angoulvant initiated the policy of so-called active penetration—in plain language, military conquest. A simple permutation: I no longer come in before the guns, but afterwards. I have gone from the vanguard to the supply corps. What can you expect? Those are the ups and downs of diplomacy."

He fell silent and looked at me, watching for my reactions. He must have been reproaching himself for saying too much. Who was I, after all, in his eyes? Doubtless some drawing-room naturalist, too young for the mission given him, whose career owed more to his society connections than to any real scientific competence. A privileged person to whom he, an obscure autodidact, had imprudently confided his own desperate ambition, an ambition aided only by his intelligence and capacity for work, and characterized by a mixture of idealism and calculation, right down to the cold liberalism of his civilizing philosophy. More serious, for the diplomat he claimed to be, he had let me see the bitterness of a disappointed careerist, which had engendered criticisms barely veiled by disciplined habits and the discreet irony of an apparent resignation. I remained silent, reading in his eyes a rising irritation and uneasiness.

"Don't misunderstand me," he began with a forced smile.

"It seems to me that no misunderstanding is possible. You have said some extremely reasonable things. In my opinion, any person who speaks more than ten languages should be appointed governor. And besides, between the two of us, I am very ill-informed about the details of colonial politics. I am essentially interested in primates."

My levity, which I meant to be reassuring, seemed for a moment to dumbfound him. Then, taking it as an insult to his own seriousness, as an insolent manifestation of a socially determined breeziness he loathed, he became icily polite and impersonal.

We arrived at a quay built on the lagoon. A small, shallow draft vessel that provided service between Grand Bassam and Abidjan was at the dock, steam up, ready to leave. My baggage was brought aboard. Blanchot accompanied me to the gangplank.

"Please give my respects to the governor, and tell him that everything is going well here."

He bowed stiffly without shaking hands, abruptly turned around, and headed hurriedly back to the city, leaving his men and the cart behind. The captain of the ship came up to me and saluted. He was a colossus, jovial and rather dilapidated.

"Welcome aboard, sir. We were waiting only for you before leaving. Blanchot's orders, the little rat. Didn't like that. Only one master on board. But I'm fond of my command and my lagoon, and that man's as powerful as he is cunning. Did he bore you with his Africans?"

"He seemed to me a remarkable man."

"Possibly. I don't understand all of his subtleties. For me, when a person—or a nation, it's the same thing—wants to dominate another, there's only one solution: a stick, sir, a big stick. What do you say?"

"Not much, Captain. In any case, it is a branch of universal pragmatic philosophy. And I suggest you apply it to your engine, so that we can arrive in Abidjan before nightfall."

"Are you giving me an order, sir? On my own ship?"

"Not at all, Captain. It was simply a suggestion."

He seemed to reflect weightily on what he should do. Finally, whether out of prudence or goodheartedness, he decided to look at the matter on the bright side.

"That's better, sir. By the way, you've got it all wrong about this engine business. You see, my engine is the only person in the world I respect. What do you say?"

"You are certainly set on knowing my thoughts, Captain. I say simply that such a person is very fortunate."

He let out a rasping laugh, a rather ridiculous sound coming from such a mass of fat and muscle. I began to feel a certain annoyance. Luckily enough, he turned on his heels, exclaiming between two high-pitched cackles, "Damn fellow! Damn fellow!"

We started off. Thinking probably that he had emerged

with his honor intact from a conversation he should not have started, and not being interested in repeating the experience, the captain did not say another word to me, for which he had my gratitude. The ship went around to the south of Désirée Island, and soon came into the stretch of water separating the continent from Petit Bassam Island. Landscapes of shrubbery, palm groves, and open forest followed one another. There was not a breath of wind, but in the distance the leaves seemed to move in an illogical, disorganized fashion, distorted by the effect of layers of overheated air that came between the eye and the shore. The forward motion of the ship created a caressing breeze too weak to cool one off or even dry the sweat that drenched one's body and soaked one's clothing. The captain was dripping, which did not seem to bother him in the least, and leaving behind him something like the nauseating track of an enormous snail. His every gesture rained down a spray that caught the light and soon evaporated on scorching contact with the deck or the steel plates of the ship's freeboard. He was from all points of view an admirable brute, as serene in a guise in which anyone else would have felt ridiculous and ugly as he was in the innocent and comic violence of his view of the world. He yelled orders studded with blasphemies and his strange little laugh. I came to wonder which, he or Africa, constituted the more surprising spectacle. At one point I pulled a bottle of whiskey out of the canvas bag hanging from my shoulder and took a swallow. The captain was passing by me and slowed down, his eyes riveted on the bottle. I handed it to him. He grabbed it, poured half its contents down his throat in a single gulp, and gave it back to me.

"Sir," he said, "anyone who drinks alcohol of such quality as nonchalantly as you do must be, as far as I am concerned, either an ignorant barbarian or a perfect gentleman. You will note that I myself am neither. This is clearly an obstacle between us. What do you say?"

"I don't see anything particularly dramatic about it. However, I think it preferable to leave the matter there."

"I wonder, sir, if at the very base of your character there isn't some kind of contempt."

"The word is a bit excessive, deduced from a relationship limited to the exchange of a few phrases and a bit of alcohol. Let us say simply that I am not drawn to you in the least."

"That's fair, sir. Exactly what I myself feel. Excuse me now, I must return to my duties."

And he headed off toward the wheel, with the sure-footed and rolling gait typical of the consummate sailor and the confirmed drunkard united in one man.

We soon arrived in sight of the headland, with its bays on either side, where Abidjan, the new capital of the colony, was being built. The ship entered the channel which separated its southern coast from the northwest tip of Petit Bassam Island, went around the cape, turning to starboard, and came to land at a brand-new dock, the only nearly completed section of an enormous port construction site, barely begun and practically abandoned, suggesting an ambition that had spent itself early.

A personage with an air of contemplative, nearly melancholy dignity, accompanied by several notables and by a military escort lined up in strict hierarchical order behind him, was waiting beyond the wharf. To judge from the evidence, this was the governor. I hoped, without much conviction, that he was there to greet another visitor, and I looked around for something resembling a brass band, which fortunately I was unable to find. In fact, it was the governor, and indeed he was waiting for me. He deigned to take several steps in my direction and approached me with perfect courtesy combined with some inexplicable emotion. The captain, high on the bridge, made a rather inane and ostentatious military salute, a gesture calculated to express as much derision tempered by prudence as respect. The governor replied with a rapid and annoyed wave, in harmony with the courtesy of the sailor and designed above all to remove that irksome apparition from a heretofore calm horizon.

"The colony," he disclosed to me half smiling, "would just as soon do without the services of that braggart. Unfortunately, he is the only one who can navigate in the lagoon without running aground."

After extended and formal introductions that gave me the feeling of being on an official visit to some subprefecture at home, our troop set out and left the phantom port. We made a brief visit to the railroad station, of which my companions seemed very proud, and arrived at the governor's new residence, situated a short distance to the north. I was given two very comfortable rooms in the east wing. I installed myself in the brighter one, having piled my baggage in the other. Then I took a bath and dressed for dinner. Someone knocked on my door. It was the governor.

"I hope I am not disturbing you," he said. "I wanted to see you privately. Please don't take offense at my question . . ."

He fell silent, looking at me with a gaze both searching and absent, and a strange smile, as if suddenly I had ceased to be an interlocutor and become a curious object, the inanimate cause of some obscure reverie.

"It seems to me," I said with a touch of impatience, "that in order to form an opinion, it would not be superfluous for me to hear the question."

He appeared to come back to himself and begged me to excuse him. Then he repeated several times, with visible emotion, my mother's first and last name, as well as her maiden name, and asked me if I were her son. Torn between curiosity and a certain reserve regarding the confidences that were sure to follow and that, coming from a stranger, might be embarrassing, I hesitated to answer, or at least to answer truthfully. However, I made up my mind to do so.

"I suspected as much," he said, "without really believing in such a coincidence, when I first read the mail from the Ministry and the Museum. It became a certainty when I saw you at the wharf. You are the living image of her. It was almost like seeing her, suddenly, after more than a quarter of a century."

I then understood the welcome he had given me, which both in administrative pomp and emotional content had seemed to me a bit out of place, and had led me to think that he no doubt set above all other human occupations the modest profession of naturalist.

"I owe you an explanation," he continued. "I knew your mother at the university. She was remarkably beautiful, and with a mind so brilliant that it heightened her beauty. But her brilliance was that of a cold light. We were all in love with her, not without a certain fear for our intellectual dignity. I was assuredly the most in love, and the most terrified. If she noticed, she never showed it. She did not in the least share this passion, and the only one I knew her to feel was for her studies. By all accounts, it took a mind surer and more agile than my own to turn her away from them and attract her attention."

"I'm dreadfully sorry for you."

"I can see," he said smiling, "that you have inherited more than her features. You have no idea how her charming irony delighted and tortured me. I would have preferred malice. That at least grants one a semblance of existence. With her, I had the feeling I did not exist, or only barely. Yet, when I left the university to follow other paths, she said to me, with a gravity I would never have expected, indeed a real sadness, 'I will miss you.' But at the same time, it was the ultimate proof that she felt no love for me. I never saw her again. Years later I learned from a common acquaintance that she had married and had a son. Our separation has stayed in my mind like a delightful and incurable tumor. It makes itself felt all the more here, in my isolation and exile. I accepted this post and I apply myself conscientiously to my duty. But I have no conviction. Blanchot, whom no doubt you met at Grand Bassam, is certainly more competent than I, but he lacked political connections. I have the impression of being just as awkward and out of place here as I was in the company of your mother. She was a mystery, a kind of Africa before its time."

He fell silent again, but continued to stare at me. I was moved and irritated by the solitude and the passion of this man. And doubtless I was irritated because I was moved; because all of this, from an earlier time, had a density and a life that touched me; because, thanks to an accident of geography, this governor, incongruous and bashful, wished to implicate me in a love that would remain until his death a splendid sketch, richer, more beautiful, and more intact than any finished work that exhausts its subject. I had to put an end to this discomfort.

"Be assured, sir, that I do not doubt your sentiments for an instant, but your portrait of my mother is rather literary, hence necessarily inexact, owing to that excessive coherence which is the mark of daydreams, and . . . how shall I say it . . . it is also a bit bloodless. I myself do not see her that way. But it is possible that my own view of her is also romanticized, based on my certainty of being the only man she ever loved. I can tolerate the idea, however, that such a certainty may be no more than a pure and simple belief. In any case, I know she is a woman, and by that I mean not only a goddess or a mother, to use a worn expression."

He remained silent. The thought came to me suddenly that he was asking himself about the precise meaning of my last words, whose ambiguity now struck me, without prompting in me any desire to clear it up. I blamed myself only for the dryness of my speech and its excessive length. He seemed lost in some kind of vague happiness. There was no way out. I stood up and opened the door, saying to him, "Permit me to finish unpacking."

He smiled and left the room. I remained thoughtful, going over in my mind the several rather strange encounters I had had in the course of the previous hours, since my arrival on African soil. I wondered if I had not made a mistake in my mission and if it might not be advisable to trade my naturalist's gear for something more suitable to the circumstances, that of an anthropologist, a novelist, or a moral philosopher, if one can consider these last two occupations as serious specialties. It did not then occur to me that in the eyes of all these people I was doubtless rather curious myself, and having first attracted their sympathy and desire to confide in me, I had succeeded, with remarkable consistency, in provoking their hostility, and had given them a rather forbidding sample of a France rendered sublime in their eyes by dream and distance.

Dinner was, if not pleasant, at least instructive. The governor had invited to his table all that Abidjan had to offer in the way of notables, whether political, administrative, economic, or financial. I was soon up to date on every issue being discussed in the colony, and was asked a multitude of questions about France, particularly its capital, as well as about European alliances and the eventuality of a war. The governor himself participated very little in the conversation. After asking details of my itinerary and the exact location where I intended to establish my base camp, he suggested I could shorten my hike by taking the train north. He said he would introduce me to a guide the following morning.

"Along with Blanchot, he is unquestionably the person who knows the country best. He took part in most of the explorations carried out during the last quarter of a century. I consider him very efficient and trustworthy. Unfortunately, he is rude, though intelligent and even cultivated. You will see if you can come to an understanding with him. I should also point out that you will perhaps meet an English expedition of the same kind as yours, which, with the consent of the Ministry, I authorized to enter our territory. The request was transmitted to me some time ago by the authorities of the Gold Coast. I presume that these people must already be in place, in the Dan country. The expedition seems important, with several Europeans and many natives. It will no doubt give you some scientific competition. The group is led by a very influential young woman, Lady Jane Savile, a famous biologist and the widow of a lord."

"Isn't she better known in scientific circles under her maiden name, Jane Sheldon?"

"That's the one. I believe that the eagerness in our authorities' letters about you is not unrelated to this British initiative. We could not refuse that courtesy to an ally, but not let them have a go at it alone, either."

After this exchange, which interested me greatly, though it vexed me a bit, the governor fell completely silent. Every time I turned toward him, I met his glance, full of an eloquent melancholy, and the discomfort I had felt in my room came over me again. To rid myself of it, I began to flirt with the woman next to me, the wife of an engineer busy with railroad work in the north and forced by his job to reside temporarily in Bouaké. About thirty years old, she was rather attractive, plump, with a pale and delicate complexion that clearly attested a desperate fastidiousness in protecting her skin from the assaults of the tropical sun. She talked to me about her husband, whom she was to join the following day, and about the fascination wrought upon her by a storybook Africa; her forced enthusiasm drowned the meaning of her words beneath that conveyed by her highly studied voice and expressions, a stylistic performance that turned the epic of the railroad into a veritable enterprise of seduction. I concluded finally that at heart she had as little taste for the place as for the person. This rhetoric led her naturally to my bed, where she remained, without meaning any harm, until dawn.

In the morning, the governor led me to a ground-floor office where he introduced a certain Jules Lefèvre, whom he proposed as my guide. Lefèvre was a short, stocky man, bald and remarkably ugly, with inscrutable features and sunken eyes that were nervously or aggressively restless, like those of a creature at the same time being stalked and preparing to attack. His dress was slovenly, and he himself only questionably clean. This vision did not enchant me in the least, and the governor, who must have read the instinctive repulsion in my face, nodded his head slightly in a conciliatory gesture. Then he left us. Lefèvre was watching me. He laughed derisively.

"You look like a very proper young man. But there must be a defect in your education. You should have been taught to hide your feelings better. What you think of me . . ."

"For the moment, I don't think anything of you, other than that you do not care much about your appearance, which seems to be obvious. However that may be, we are not here to talk about my feelings, but about yours, concerning this expedition. I want to set up my base camp on the right side of the upper Sassandra, not far from the Toura and Dan massifs. I have learned that it is there that one finds the largest chimpanzee populations. Our stay will last for several months."

"I am interested. I know the region well, and I

believe," he said, looking at me ironically, "that my presence might not be superfluous. Appearances don't count in the jungle. You will learn that rather quickly. My conditions are the following: a respectable salary, paid punctually every week in cash. Rest on Sunday. Absolute freedom of decision in matters concerning the itinerary and relations with the natives. As much whiskey as I want. And a little consideration."

I could not help laughing, which lightened the atmosphere.

"Here are mine," I said. "I think that I am intelligent enough to recognize the limits of my competence. Within those limits, you will obey my orders."

We rapidly agreed on his salary. Then I talked to him about the governor's suggestion that we take the railroad.

"There are three possible routes," he said. "Reaching the Sassandra by boat and going up the river, which would be very long. Or, in fact, taking the train. The railroad reached Bouaké last year. Bouaké is, as the crow flies, the closest station to the Dan country. But this is also the most dangerous route, and the least well known. I propose a third solution, a sort of compromise. Take the train, get off at Dimbokro, reach the junction of the Bandama and the Marahoué, a tributary, by going across Baoulé territory; follow the Marahoué into Gouro country, then head straight west to the Sassandra. It's the easiest route, except for the last part, which goes through a dense jungle between the two rivers. It should also, theoretically, enable us to avoid hostile natives."

"So be it. Will three days be enough time to prepare?"

"Easily. I would like to have a look at your equipment, so that I can determine the number of porters to hire."

I led him to my rooms. He quickly evaluated the volume and weight of my baggage, remarked on the excessive quantity of clothing, and asked to see the weapons. I showed him an automatic pistol.

"Rather nice," he said. "A model 3 Walther, 1910, 7.65 caliber."

He added that he preferred revolvers, because of problems with the safety and the compression of the spring on the catch that were a matter of complete indifference to me.

"Is that all?"

"Yes."

He again let out that derisive laugh which showed much more cynicism than gaiety.

"You really don't know what you are up against. Plunging into the jungle with a hand weapon . . ."

"I never thought to go there alone. My intention is to observe, not to kill anyone or anything. That, should the occasion arise, will be your job."

"Nonetheless, I will get you a 7x57 caliber—in plain language, a Mauser 7mm rifle. One never knows. You will perhaps be forced to dirty your hands. Let's sum up. If we add to your kit and mine the provisions we won't be able to find on the way, we will need about ten porters. Rendezvous here in three days, two hours before the train leaves. I will have the suppliers' bills delivered to you. If you need to contact me, you will find me in the evenings at Henri's, a bar near the railroad station. Don't come too late, if you want to have a serious conversation, and I don't very well see what other kind of conversation you could have. When I am not in the jungle, I am drunk every night beginning at 9:00 P.M."

"And at what time are you drunk in the jungle?"

He gazed at me for a moment. He smiled in an almost pleasant way, turned on his heels, said "Good-bye, sir," and left. I was tempted to go after him and say to hell with our contract. But he had convinced me, despite my aversion to him, of his knowledge of the country and his organizational efficiency and decisiveness. I had to recognize in him a certain shrewdness and a brutal frankness likely to simplify our relations, which I decided to limit to the strictly necessary. I was afraid, however, that I would not be able to overcome my antipathy. Rarely had a being so displeased me at first sight. His obvious disgust with the world came perhaps from a secret disgust with himself, for his shrewdness must also have applied to his own person. If he had immediately noticed my recoiling before his misery, his ugliness, and above all that sort of hate emanating from his face, it must have been because he expected it and to a certain extent found it natural, even provoked and aggravated it, insolently and ostentatiously decking himself out in all the outward signs of a pariah. After all, I said to myself to get this character out of my mind, it is possible that a nasty and dismal buffoon in the city can make a perfectly presentable guide in the woods.

With impatience, I caught myself again practicing a kind of psychology which, as a scientist, I ordinarily mistrusted. It was probably an uncatalogued African illness.

I spent the following three days preparing the expedition and politely avoiding the governor's fits of nostalgic sociability. I feared he was developing a kind of sentimental, not to say amorous, fixation on me, not because of my own merits or personal charm, but, on the contrary, because, in his eyes, I reproduced the maternal phenotype in the most striking fashion, considering my maleness and in spite of it, that is, give or take a few details. I wrote a note of reproach to my mother on this subject, saying that while she had warned me at length against all the calamities careful research had suggested to her, among them wild beasts, beverage abuse, amebiasis, dysentery, and malaria, she had not added to her interminable list—whether unwittingly or out of a taste for secrecy—the danger posed by her former admirers posted in the subequatorial zone.

The morning of our departure, at 7:00, Lefèvre appeared at the conciergerie of the residence accompanied by ten solid Abidji, seven of whom were rather heavily loaded. The three others came to get my own baggage, and we made our way to the railroad station. The governor insisted on accompanying me. He exempted us from buying tickets and divided us up in the train according to a discriminatory principle which indicated the absolute clarity, down to the slightest detail, of his hierarchical vision of the social universe:

the equipment in the rear baggage car; the porters in third class, where the cars were filled with a noisy and joyous crowd; Lefèvre in second class, among troops returning north after leave in Abidjan, and myself in a comfortable first-class car empty of other passengers. He made urgent recommendations to Lefèvre, which put me ill at ease and brought a mocking grin to the lips of the guide.

"Don't be afraid, sir, I will take infinite care of your protégé."

He said these last words with contained scorn, and looking at me in a way that put me into a cold fury. I would have liked to wring both their necks.

For two hours the train had been going along slowly. The continual whispering of its steam engine was punctuated by whistle blasts of varying length, whose usefulness or logic I could not understand, and which I ultimately attributed to the whim of the engineer. After frequent stops near the plantations in the lagoon area, the train entered the dense jungle. On both sides of the embankment, the hygrophilous forest raised an impenetrable wall of colossal vegetation. It was like an ocean mounted on pilings. On the ground, nearly bare because of the scarcity of light, enormous tree trunks, bereft of lower branches and tangled with interlacings of vines and stilt roots, rose up in the midst of a semi-darkness saturated with water, and supported a sea of foliage whose green waves broke thirty meters from the bottom. Here and there, islands surfaced in the light, giant species dominating with their vertiginous plumes the infinite swell from which they emerged. On the edges of this mantle, where the sun struck the base of the trunks, the delicate gleichenia grew beneath the open sky, a froth of ferns underscoring with their fringe the narrow unwooded coastline. It was a curiously peaceful shore, under the still menace of the jungle, a monstrous groundswell stopped just as it was about to break. For the first time since my arrival I felt physically the assault of an incomparable savagery. And yet, I was sheltered in a small piece of Europe, a comfortably furnished space that took away from this primitive and carnivorous luxuriance part of its reality. I tried to imagine the moment when, practically unarmed and naked, I would have to penetrate that moist genesis, to detect the diversity, the order, and the reason behind this mask of profuse monotony, chaos, and insanity, to integrate myself into that which offered the purest image of strangeness.

After a one-hour stop at Agboville, a town of small houses endowed with some European-style buildings and a stationmaster so meticulously and determinedly French-looking that he alone called into question the authenticity of the landscape, the train plunged into less dense jungle and arrived at Dimbokro toward the end of the afternoon. During the animated unloading, Lefèvre showed a sense of organization that was rather brutal, but unquestionably efficient. Managing as best we could, we spent the night in the house and outbuildings of an acquaintance of the governor, an obliging but taciturn man who had been forewarned of our arrival and with whom we did not exchange ten sentences. The next day, shortly before dawn, we made a final check and divided up the equipment according to the strength and endurance of each person. After brief farewells to our host, with the guide leading the way and myself taking up the rear, an arrangement that put between us the distance of our ten porters and thus did not displease me, we entered the suffocating heat of the jungle. We headed west-northwest, toward the junction of the Bandama and the Marahoué.

The appearance of the landscape no longer presented exactly the same characteristics I had observed from the train before arriving in Agboville. There were fewer vines, and the stilt roots had disappeared. The trunks, thus freed, seemed more willowy and gracious in their thrust. The sun's rays managed to penetrate the undergrowth, allowing an uneven carpet of grass to cover the ground. The samba and the Gabon tulip tree, loaded down with its red flowers, competed for space. The makore became less dense as we proceeded west. The nettle trees were abundant. The mesophytic forest extended as far as the eye could see, expressing all the nuances of the confrontation between the Tropic of Cancer and the equator.

Lefèvre walked at a sure and steady pace. From time to time he turned back toward the column, and I was surprised to see a jubilant air imprinting an almost childlike look on his ravaged features. He was a Gorgon decked out in an amiable grin. The porters advanced effortlessly, with longer and more harmonious strides, as if their loads, whose existence one could discern only from a certain stiffness in their bearing, weighed almost nothing. Without turning their heads, they occasionally exchanged words that provoked laughter. My stride was as long as that of the largest of them, and twice Lefèvre's, but because of the heat, this strolling pace was taking on the character of a forced march. I felt neither muscle fatigue nor breathlessness, but the sweat that trickled down my body and my face, at times even blinding me, made me exasperatingly uncomfortable. In spite of my thirst, I decided to drink only when we rested, and then with moderation, waiting until we made camp to completely rehydrate my system, from which water was being squeezed as from a sponge. This method proved successful, and in the evening I arrived in a reasonably decent state at the place chosen by Lefèvre for our camp, which earned me a brief glance of approval from the guide. He had our four tents, which were large enough to stand up in, pitched around a fire. Two were reserved for the Abidji, who had to pile into them as best they could, spreading blankets over a thick bed of greenery to protect themselves from the water seeping in. Ours were equipped with basic furniture, including a camp bed with mosquito net, a portable table and chair, and an alcohol lamp. Dinner was dispatched in almost total silence. Lefèvre and I had nothing to say to each other, and the porters glanced at us furtively, doubtless confused by this coldness, intrigued by an obvious absence of the solidarity which, among them, seemed total. I remarked to myself that we were giving them an exact image of Europe. The guide stood up and assigned the guard watches, from which he excluded me, among the ten porters and himself. I supposed that he wanted thereby to spare me additional fatigue, or that he lacked confidence in my ability to interpret jungle noises. I lay down on my bed. I could not fall asleep; I was extremely enervated by the heat and by strong impressions of the trip that I could not share with anyone because of the silence and solitude imposed by my aversion to Lefèvre, an aversion he himself seemed to foster. A little later, I heard him in his tent noisily droning out this curious bit of a hymn, which seemed an exact enough reflection of his general state of mind:

> *Everybody stinks and stinks and stinks*
> *Just like rotting meat.*
> *It's only, only, only my Jesus*
> *Who smells fresh and sweet.*

These laughable devotions sounded vaguely familiar to me, and I remembered having seen them quoted by Hugo in his chronicle of the Channel Islands. I wondered whether Lefèvre owed his knowledge of this piece of pessimistic eloquence to a Huguenot heritage or to a surprising interest in literature.

Towards midnight, a torrential rain began to fall. I stepped out of my tent and was drenched in an instant by a stream of warm water. I stood there, motionless in the storm. One of the Abidji, dressed in a simple loincloth and leaning on his rifle, was crouching in front of the fire, which was reduced to a few dead coals lying in a blackish mud of ashes soaked by the downpour. From time to time he half disappeared, hidden by an opaque wall of rain. He was a blind and absurd lookout, a watchman over nothingness. One could hear the jungle drinking.

The next day we reached the outer edge of the dense forest and entered a sea of graminae which marked the beginning of a hybrid and more open landscape, a mixture of savannah and open forest, where the grassy expanse was dotted with neré, irokos, and palmyra palms sprouting in abundance. Infiltrations of forest arcades, narrow columns of dense vegetation that the jungle sent out to storm the savannah, and islets of thick woods besieged by the low waves of graminae were like indomitable bastions of the mesophytic world persisting on foreign soil.

At the end of three days' march through the monotony of this landscape, we arrived at the banks of the Bandama a bit downstream from the junction, and set up camp on a knoll near a little beach. It was Saturday. The next day would be a day of rest. According to the

terms of the contract, I paid Lefèvre and the porters
their first week's salary. The guide insisted on drawing
up a receipt on which each one of them, opposite his
name, written out in capital letters, had to put his
mark—a comic administrative detail followed by a gulp
of whiskey designed to give the matter indispensable
emphasis.

After dinner, which was a bit more lively than usual,
Lefèvre took a bottle of alcohol out of a chest. A porter,
whose reserve with regard to us had probably been
overcome by the day's unusual agenda, turned to me
with a big smile, and indicating the guide with a nod of
the head, pointed his thumb at his throat in a gesture
of drinking, as if he found this fun irresistible. Lefèvre
saw him. In the calmest possible way he went to cut a
branch, whose leaves he carefully began to remove as
he approached the joker.

"I advise you," I said to him, "to find another use for
that piece of wood quickly, if you want to avoid losing
face."

He stopped and looked at me with an expression of
surprise that slowly changed to anger.

"Our contract," he said between his teeth, "leaves me
total freedom with regard to the natives. You are
breaking it by preventing me from correcting the insolence of an inferior. Your showy liberalism may prove
to be dangerous."

"As far as I am concerned, this inferiority matter is
not a question of morality, but of anthropology. It

therefore does not fall outside the domain of my modest competence. And in that case, our contract stipulates that you are to obey my orders."

Lefèvre threw the branch into the fire and went into his tent, violently pulling down its canvas door. "Not too bad a way out," I said to myself, looking at the green wood that twisted and whistled in the fire, its sap boiling. The Abidji were watching me, doubtless having understood not one word of our brief exchange, but intrigued by this business of the branch. I went and lay down on my bed. I was almost pleased with our altercation, which had broken the oppressive silence.

This explosion had the merit of freeing our spirits for a while from the stormy weight that had accumulated day after day. The following morning, Lefèvre proved to be nearly cheerful, no doubt to avoid recalling the previous night's scene, or at least to treat it as harmless after the fact. Apparently he preferred reconciliation to murder.

The afternoon was devoted to the construction of two large rafts, made of tree trunks bound with ropes and supported by crosspieces, capable of carrying all the men and equipment in one trip.

We embarked on Monday at daybreak, Lefèvre in command of the first raft, I of the second, at a respectful distance from the junction of the two rivers, in order to avoid the eddies where the waters came together. The Bandama, however, swollen by the Marahoué and the recent storms, had a stronger current than its calm surface led us to believe, and we came to a point where the depth of the riverbed made our poles useless, either for pushing or for steering. We started to drift, making no appreciable progress towards the other shore and losing considerable ground downstream. The Abidji began to show signs of uneasiness.

The guide yelled to me:

"There's a rough passage a bit further down. We have to reach land before that, or we risk capsizing."

"Do you know how to swim?"

"Good God, no! No one knows how to swim here."

Some twenty meters away, the riverbank was passing, close and unattainable. I threw Lefèvre a rope and ordered him to tie the rafts together. Then I picked up another, the longest we had, bound one end to a crosspiece and the other around my waist, took off my boots, and jumped in. I began to swim as hard as I could, without trying to struggle against the current, moving away from the rafts while still following their drift, in order to prevent the tow rope from becoming taut, which would have resulted in my being dragged along and losing control of my movements. I hoisted myself up on the bank, removed the rope, and tied it around a tree. There was a sharp tug. The rafts stopped, heads down in the current, and were washed over their entire length by a respectable quantity of water that nearly upset them and their passengers. They regained their stability and were carried along towards the shore, where they landed shortly thereafter. The equipment was quickly unloaded and put away. Lefèvre came up to me, looking gloomy.

"I made a mistake, and acted rashly. I will never forgive myself for letting you do my work."

"It seems to me that it is sometimes necessary to take certain liberties with contracts. I had to try something to save your whiskey. By the way, I would gladly have a swallow."

An hour later we reached the junction and began to proceed up the right bank of the Marahoué, whose upstream waters vanished in the northwest.

"We are leaving Baoulé territory and entering Gouro country," Lefèvre told me. "In theory, these people are not hostile. But I prefer to avoid the villages."

After three days' march along the river without any incident of note, the guide announced that we had arrived at the exact latitude of the Dan country, and would no longer follow the Marahoué, but head straight west, through the dense jungle, towards the Sassandra. We plunged again into the mesophytic forest, which as we traveled west became ever thicker and wetter. We walked in an endless twilight, and the heavy soil became bare for lack of light. Dominating other more adaptable species, which had remained here and there in the galleries and wooded islands of the pre-forest savannah, the makore now returned in strength and splendor. Torrential rains, pouring through a massive roof of ferns that scattered their fall, flooded this gigantic sanctuary, whose vegetable altars were decorated with red, violet, and white flowers. In the thickest areas vines appeared, colonies of epiphytes covered trunks and branches, and certain species protected themselves from the dampness of the water-soaked earth by a vast network of creeping roots. During dry periods, evaporation produced a suffocating veil of moisture that clouded one's perceptions and put up against our march a kind of liquid resistance.

The following Saturday, at the end of the day, we arrived, exhausted, at the banks of the Sassandra. In the west, reddened by the light of sunset, the halo-ringed Man mountains filled the horizon, dominating a tide of greenery thrown up against their slopes.

"Dan country is on the other side of the river," said the guide. "Same orders as for the Gouro. It's preferable to avoid the inhabited areas. The Dan are not particularly hostile to us, but they are rather warlike. Besides, the two tribes have the same origin. They both come from the Mandé country, in the northwest."

After the salary payment ritual, we had a quick dinner and a rest that lasted late into Sunday morning. In the afternoon, Lefèvre directed the construction of the rafts that would take us across the Sassandra. This time he did not want to omit any precaution. The first boat was light and long, of a design that would assure its easy maneuverability. The second, much larger and more stable, was built to support a heavy load. We cut poles five meters long, in order to avoid losing contact with the bottom, as had happened when we crossed the Bandama. On Monday at dawn, four Abidji and I boarded the smaller craft. A rope long enough to join the two banks was attached to its stern and to the prow of the larger raft. We crossed the river quickly and easily. Lefèvre, having loaded all the equipment on the other boat, got on board, followed by the last six porters. They began to push on their poles with a conviction that betrayed an obvious nervousness and provoked an outburst of sarcastic good humor among my companions, who were now out of danger. We settled down to hauling on the tow-rope, which we pulled in slowly and steadily. In spite of a slight drift, the raft soon came ashore without mishap. The guide decided to go upstream along the riverbank to a place he knew to be particularly well suited for setting up a permanent base camp, from which our expeditions would leave for the nearby monkey territory. We arrived to discover that someone had preceded us. A vast semicircular stockade had been built from stakes three meters long, driven into the ground at one-foot intervals, with long flexible poles interwoven horizontally to ensure their strength and solidity. Here and there narrow slits had been made to serve as loopholes. At the ends of this semicircle, open on the Sassandra, the last stakes were planted in the riverbed itself. In the middle, facing the jungle, was an opening that could be masked by a hingeless door, solid and heavy, not yet put in place for the night. On the inside, flanking a central pathway that led from the entrance to an indentation in the riverbank—a sort of rocky beach whose gentle slope allowed easy access to the water—a dozen tents were pitched, four to the south, the largest set apart from the others, and eight to the north. There was probably, in this colonial city in miniature, a European quarter and an African quarter.

Jungles

In spite of the warlike and methodical appearance of this fortress, which reminded one of a military camp, I had no doubt that, by accident or necessity, I had come upon the English scientific expedition about which the governor had spoken.

"I insist, Henry, although I am perfectly aware that by so doing I offer an easy target for that cynicism which is yours as a man of the world and a scientist—since it is always easier to take nothing seriously—I insist that literature is the highest manifestation of the human spirit, and that Art in general is what distinguishes mankind absolutely and definitively from all other living things. Art is not an accident in the evolution of a species, a sophisticated phenomenon of adaptation, as you claim, but an end in itself, that which gives coherence and motivation to

a universe that without it would be doomed to absurdity."

This rather banal profession of faith took on an
incongruous air, proclaimed in the midst of the jungle
like a counterpoint to the primitive eloquence of the
African night. There were six of us around a table set
up in the middle of the camp, a kind of country dining
room, lit by kerosene lamps, open to the four winds,
protected only by a vast two-sided roof of palm branches.
We were served by natives of the Gold Coast, whose
strange get-up consisted of incomplete liveries that
contrasted with their calloused and bush-worn bare feet.
After two weeks in the jungle, all of this, in addition to
the content of the conversation and the fact that it was
a formal dinner our hosts had improvised in honor of
our arrival, rather our irruption, seemed a delectable
anomaly to me. I was seated at the right of the head of
the English expedition, Lady Savile, or Jane Sheldon if
you prefer, who was at the end of the table. She must
have been about thirty years old, or a bit more, and was
one of those Anglo-Saxons of whom Gregory the Great
could have said *Non Angli, sed angeli*. This angel, at first
glance, seemed to be made more of marble than flesh.
Everything in her bearing, gestures, expressions, the
tone of her voice, was imbued with that untroubled
authority, that distant and flawless assurance, that gracious and detached superiority, carried like a kind of
natural and intangible principle, which the combination
of birth, beauty, and knowledge sometimes bestows
upon individuals above all modesty and vanity. And the

dazzled spectator could come to suspect, behind this appearance of cold perfection, a somewhat defiling passion. On her left, opposite me, was her assistant, Henry Sterne, a solid and attractive man, cheerful and full of an irony that sometimes verged on total skepticism. This skepticism was not of the sort which acts as a more or less philosophical defense by an individual to justify his incompetence in the face of all the dizzying possibilities of knowledge—a common enough thing in quite a few cramped minds frustrated by their own laziness—but, on the contrary, was based on a breathtakingly extensive culture. My neighbor was Samuel Fielding, the guide of the English expedition, an affable and good-tempered giant, a kind of gentleman farmer with a levelheaded taste for adventure, as much at ease in the boundless African forest as in the ordered countryside of his native Suffolk. He was a man who cultivated a tolerant distrust of abstractions and a pragmatism so resolute that it seemed a constant manifestation of his sense of humor. Opposite him, on Sterne's left, was seated Lefèvre, reserved, but curiously interested in the conversation, which led me to believe that the man had resources still unknown to me. At the far end of the table sat Laurence Richardson, Lady Savile's secretary, a poet and writer, a pale good-looking young man who seemed descended in a direct line from the romantic universe of the previous century. It was he who had just flung out as food for Sterne's irony this courageous and fiery declaration about Eternal Art.

"That smells of bigotry from twenty feet away,"

replied Sterne with an amiable smile. "Follow your idea right to its conclusion, my dear Laurence, and say that Art is proof of an anthropomorphic God, or at least an anthropocentric one."

"It is not a question of that, but of the irreducible and incomparable nature of artistic creation."

"Then we must admit that you are reasoning like Pangloss. That worthy fellow maintained that everything being for the best and nothing being due to chance, noses were created only for holding up eyeglasses. That would mean that the transcendental subject, in Kant's sense, is eyeglasses, mystical preliminaries to the vulgar instrument, the nose, whose necessity they introduce."

"I don't see the connection."

"But it seems evident to me. If, as you maintain, Art is an end in itself, giving coherence and motivation to the universe, then that reduces us, hominid primates, to the role of simple instruments of Art, and would indicate that we were made only for its necessary accomplishment. We had to exist, because Art is. Such determinism is doubtless not biological, but it is no better than its biological counterpart. You will grant me that there is nothing there from which to draw the enthusiastic vanity you display, but, on the contrary, everything to provoke extreme humility. Unless you admit that the instrument itself is contaminated by the great purpose it serves, which would be the same as saying that a paintbrush, a simple combination of wood and bristles, has the right to acquire who knows what metaphysical quality from the fact of the immaterial perfection of the picture."

"My God, Henry, you are too subtle for me, and you have a talent for perverting what's evident. There is no question of dissociating Art from him who produces it."

"It is not a matter of evidence, but an act of faith."

"And what if it were? I defy you to prove to me, with your cold science and your twisted logic, that Art, completely free, sovereign, unamenable to academic reasoning—I will go so far as to say sovereign and unamenable because it is free—does not escape your biological determinism."

"You yourself would first have to prove to me the merit of the terms of your argument, that is to say that Art is unamenable to reason, sovereign and free. Those are nothing but improbable adjectives, the unfailing ingredient of all sterile discussions. Nonetheless, I am going to try to answer you. Nearly all the individuals making up our species, by virtue of the evolution of their brain and their consciousness, have a need for a vision of the world that is coherent and, if possible, purposeful, something you have just illustrated brilliantly. This necessity admitted, it seems to me that Art is only a means of cloaking ignorance."

"How dare you!" said Richardson with restrained violence. "Da Vinci was both a prodigious scientist and an artistic genius!"

"Your example is threadbare. Da Vinci, like all his contemporaries, did not know very much. At the very least, his knowledge allowed a considerable dose of imagination. But let us talk rather about the arts based on language, which is the shared medium of scientific reasoning, the philosophical essay, and works of fiction. You yourself have preferred the practice of literature. Literature, long the ally of religions to the extent that it pursued the same end—namely that purposeful vision of the world which I mentioned—and which for some time has in a way competed with them, is in my view the repository of the most remarkable banalities produced by the human mind, a mountain of fragmentary and aleatory experiences, of inanities and errors. On top of this, one is supposed to discover a unifying principle that would sanctify, as you suggested, the absoluteness of our nature, the eternity of our inventive yet undeveloped mind. I no longer know which French author said that literature is the ultimate discourse of disorder. The poor man seemed to find a positive quality in that, something like an expression of freedom. Doubtless he did not see that the disorder arose from common ignorance. Unless one imagines that a writer, by definition an individual without any specialization, has some innate insight, which brings us back to genetics. As for myself, I rather think he is a fool, at times a very talented one, who addresses himself to other fools likely to find in his wanderings some artificial and illusory benefit. I admit that literature and Art in general are a peculiarity of the evolution of the human mind, and therefore of the species, but I refuse to draw from that the slightest metaphysical conclusion. And I do not see how this peculiarity contradicts a loose definition of biological determinism."

"It seems to me," cried out Richardson, "that the interest of existence and consciousness is precisely this transcendence that you purport to despise, it is beauty, madness, passion, love, solitude, despair, the idea of death. What can account for all that constitutes man and man's freedom, your biology or literature? Has the determinism of matter killed off the divine ramblings of the spirit?"

The dialogue risked turning into an altercation, Sterne's irony becoming more biting as Richardson's irritation mounted. For the others, silent spectators, the situation became uncomfortable. Fielding intervened good-naturedly, but not without a certain humorous perfidiousness:

"Come, Laurence old boy, don't work yourself up into such a state. Any opinion is respectable in proportion to its sincerity. As far as I am concerned, I suppose the sensible attitude is to suffer as little as possible and always to have some company, so one doesn't sink into solitary melancholy. Love is not worth as much as solid affection, and death being inevitable, why go on quibbling forever? As for beauty, it seems to me the most uncertain and the most relative thing in the world. Look at the cock's crow, which we find so ungraceful and ridiculous. Well, it seems to seduce the hens. Granted, there's not much in all this to inspire literature . . ."

Richardson himself could not keep from laughing.

"I will agree with you at least on one point, Laurence," said Lady Savile. "A work of art is indeed irreducible. But I do not see any great advantage there from the point of view of thought. Scientific reasoning can be reduced, without an appreciable loss of information, often to a simple equation. But the essential information contained in a work of art is what is commonly called its style. For example, in the case of a literary work, it is the totality of its distinctive syntax. Now, if it is possible to summarize the subject of a novel in a few lines—rarely is it worth more—it is impossible to reduce its form without changing it radically. We have always known that music is a pure interplay of sounds. But can we not now think, because of the progressive disappearance of mythological content, that painting is nothing but an interplay of colors, and literature a play on words? If the only real meaning is scientific meaning, which is what I think, in that it is reducible, refutable, and subject to controlled experiments, then we must admit the complete dissociation of artistic and intellectual activity, that is to say logic, which is, with your permission dear Laurence, the true and essential attribute of mankind."

"This attribute of mankind seems very inhuman, madam," said Richardson with effort.

"You have a right to think so, and I can understand that all of this is contrary to your own scale of values. To be precise, I do not deny Art the capacity to provoke the greatest pleasures, nor its intuition, depth, or, more generally, its affective meaning, which I would oppose to real meaning. What leaves me more perplexed is specialized criticism—whether of Art or literature—that false knowledge elevated to the dignity of a discipline. Being of the same nature as its object but without possessing its virtues, it seems to me disqualified in advance, and strikes me as more parasitic than analytic. It would perhaps be more interesting—and this leads us back to your argument—to consider Art from a completely external point of view, biological for example, as a manifestation of the evolution and adaptation particular to a species both from the point of view of its modalities and of its contents."

"Do you believe," said Richardson in a toneless voice, "that my feelings for you are biological?"

"You are getting off the track, Laurence."

The secretary's face fell.

"Madam, I beg your pardon."

In view of his visible distress, I felt myself obliged to provoke a diversion.

"In my opinion, the split is not so obvious. It seems to me that there is always a certain proportionality between knowledge and imagination, between what you, madam, called real meaning and affective meaning. A man who knows nothing is a wretched dreamer. At the very least his dream runs the risk of lacking the material exactitude necessary for it to become a work of art, that is a meticulously constructed object. Imagination most often lives on the suffering of consciousness, thus, to a certain extent, on the knowledge of the law of nature. And if that law, which, all things considered, comes down to death, is intolerable for human consciousness, it is not so surprising that the imagination revolts and refuses it, that the dreamer tries to escape the dead end into which the logician has led him, or that he experiences a certain melancholy. If one is to believe Mr. Richardson, this metaphysics of refusal, or of melancholy, has become a metaphysics of its own expression, the work of art itself. As if the meaning, what he called the end in itself, had gone from the idea to the figure, the metaphor."

"My compliments, sir, on your understanding attitude," said Henry Sterne. "It seems to me, however, that this use of an empty rhetorical figure as the ultimate end, this cult of form that charms our friend Laurence, comes not so much from a rejection of the law in question as from pure and simple ignorance of it. There is doubtless a fear among our artists that all of this geometry might harm their spirit of finesse, and rather than taking the tiger by the tail, they find it simpler and more beneficial to confine themselves to avoiding it, at the risk of falling into another danger, that of talking driveling nonsense."

"Permit me to retire," said Richardson standing up. "I feel tired."

Lady Savile nodded her assent, and Richardson went away stiffly in the direction of his tent, leaving us in an embarrassed silence.

"He is wrong not to like tea," said Fielding finally. "It would do him a great deal of good. I have always thought that tea contains a stoical principle which, with the addition of milk, becomes an indispensable tonic for the sense of humor. If you permit, madam, we are going to retire also. I would like to show my distinguished French colleague the new hunting weapon Henry brought me from London."

He left the table, accompanied by Lefèvre, and they disappeared into the night.

"Your irony, Henry," said Lady Savile, in an irritated voice, "is sometimes inappropriate. I am tired of your constant verbal jousting with Laurence. You should not push things so far as to become hurtful. It seems to me that, out of simple consideration for our guests, a truce was in order for this evening. Now, thanks to you, our little reception is routed."

"I assure you, madam," I then said, "I do not feel that way about it at all. I maintain, in defense of Mr. Sterne, that even in circumstances that require the most civilized exchanges, the risks at stake in intellectual argument are always preferable to the tranquillity of the trifling. And while I have some difficulty understanding Mr. Richardson's extreme sensitivity, I am not in the slightest embarrassed by his reaction. In fact, after a fortnight in the jungle, I could not dream of a more pleasantly original welcome."

She greeted this small diplomatic effort with a smile that expressed a mixture of amusement and gratitude. Tempering the cold seduction of her features, it gave her face an air of softness, almost of abandon, which rendered still more present in the mind of the observer—by I don't know what perverse effect of contrast—the firmness of her character and the eminence of her mind, now touched all at once by a dazzling symptom of humanity. Lost in a confused reverie, I could not take my eyes off her, and she returned my gaze with quiet charm.

"I am not, madam," Sterne broke in opportunely, "as guilty as you think. Laurence can perhaps become irritated at my little rational ironies, but in my opinion they are only scratches to him. On the other hand, I believe that the smallest pointed remark, the slightest touch of disdain from you, wounds him mortally. And it was the serene clarity of your words, far more than the intemperance of my own, that put him into his present state. As Samuel would say, lack of humor, dislike for tea, excess of passion . . . All of that is hardly English."

"Well, now," said Lady Savile with cutting gaiety, "here our guest is informed, in spite of himself, of all the emotional undercurrents agitating our expedition, thanks to Laurence's confusion of mind and your insolence, Henry. Isn't one likely to think this is a sentimental journey, and not a scientific mission? On this last subject, sir, it would be more reasonable for us to combine our efforts, instead of engaging in sterile competition, since our purpose is the same. As the campsite is safe and large enough to accommodate you, I invite you to install yourselves here at your convenience, and I propose that beginning tomorrow morning we discuss together the course to be followed. We have already made several forays into chimpanzee territory, and have located a large number of populations, as well as a section of their travel routes. But until now we have not succeeded in getting close enough to observe them usefully."

I accepted her proposal with thanks. After a brief exchange on the subject, Lady Savile in turn retired. I bowed to her, and she put her hand on my forearm saying, "I am happy you have decided to stay with us."

For a brief instant I felt the firm pressure of her fingers; then she pulled away from me and went off. I watched the whiteness of her naked shoulders disappear gradually into the shadows.

"It would certainly seem," said Sterne after a rather long silence, "that Lady Savile at some point stopped considering you a scientific expedition and took into account that you are a human being."

"Your sense of humor sometimes seems impenetrable to me. But perhaps, having now no more than my modest person to sink your teeth into, you are trying to pick a quarrel with me."

He laughed lightheartedly.

"What an idea! Lower your guard a bit, sir. Are you of the same breed as Lady Savile? Or is it possible that you should so soon have been seized by that touchy sentimentality she has the art of arousing wherever she goes?"

"You are right," I said, laughing in turn. "Forgive me, and now let us drink, shall we?"

"That's the spirit. It would certainly not be proper to let this burgundy spoil in the miasma of the tropics.

Give me a minute. I'm going to invite Laurence into our restricted circle. The poor boy. I owe him that, to make amends."

I remained alone, taking in the night. One could hear the regular lapping of the Sassandra, where the full moon, rising over the foliage on the opposite bank, was reflected in silvery currents. Occasionally, the dive of some batrachian or the brief splash of a fish jumping disturbed the monotonous murmur. The smooth water was wrinkled here and there by short waves underscored by the play of white light on their peaks, the wake of some stealthy monster swimming slowly. At the edge of the river, the Abidji and the men from the Gold Coast, forming two very distinct groups, sat talking. From several tents the dull glimmer of the lamps filtered through the thick canvas, and in the largest, where the light was very bright, a slender shadow moved without hurry. From the jungle came distant cries, hoarse or strident, short or strangely echoing, a kind of violent symphony composed of ferocity and panic, expressing the monotonous horror of a never-ending slaughter. This mixture of peace close at hand and turmoil taking shape in the distance seemed an exact reflection of my own internal landscape as I contemplated the silhouette drawn by the light behind the canvas screen.

Sterne came back, accompanied by Richardson.

"Please, sir," said the latter, "forgive the foolishness of my behavior. I did not have the slightest intention of being rude. In my defense I will say that once having been as tactless as possible in the utmost sincerity, I could find no recourse but to flee. This does not put into question the firmness of my convictions, but only the meagerness of my talent in defending them."

"That is what happens, my dear Laurence," said Sterne, "when one tries to elevate to the abstract level of the aesthetic ideal the minds of hair-splitters who spend their existence counting the petals of flowers instead of taking from their ineffable beauty the elements of a universal metaphysics."

As the night and the wine flowed on, the conversation progressively brought forth the idiosyncrasy of each speaker and escaped from the rules of compromise, thanks to that vague freedom, halfway between sincerity and abandon, that a reasonable degree of intoxication commonly favors. Sterne's ironic pessimism, losing its aggressivity, became more persuasive and more revealing.

"Mr. Jack London, may God bless him, while like you, Laurence, a man of letters, does not share your prejudices with regard to biology. He has obviously a somewhat hazy approach to it, reading Darwin in the philosophical translation by Spencer. Philosophers have the deplorable habit of seeing in the restricted systems of scientists—that is, when they have the elementary honesty to consider them—the keys to universal understanding, a fact which demonstrates their mania for synthesis, their scant sensitivity to the contradictions of experiment, and, in a word, their intellectual racketeering. They are, unbeknownst to themselves, failed poets, lacking both talent and the blind generosity of pure intuition. They are one-eyed, which for me is worse than being blind. Mr. London at least does not have the pedantry to stick on his forehead that ridiculous label of 'specialist in generality.' No doubt he subordinates biology to his morality, which spares him the trouble of excessive precision, but his intention is praiseworthy and quite out of the ordinary for his profession. This man of the people has more insight than the very refined Voltaire, who in speaking of Telliamed—or rather, of Benoît de Maillet and the strange foresight about evolutionism displayed in his *Conversations of an Indian Philosopher with a French Missionary about the Lowering of the Sea*—declared 'This Telliamed seems to me slightly injured in the brain,' and thereby demonstrated the conformist foolishness of a right-thinking bourgeois."

"I am delighted," said Richardson, "to note that at least two writers, one an author of popular adventure novels and the other a complete unknown, save the profession from total stupidity. However, it seems to me that it was poor Voltaire, and not your friend Telliamed, who advised cultivating one's garden."

"Well," said Sterne, laughing, "instead of cultivating sterile varieties of ornamental species, he should have planted peas, like Gregor Mendel. Now there was a man who drew but a few lines out of the observations of an entire lifetime. Yet, in my view, those few lines will have more weight in the century that is just beginning than the great systems of Buffon, Lamarck, Darwin, and others like Weismann."

"I see with a certain jubilation that your horror of generalities pushes you to criticize your equals, not to say your betters. Might you have doubts about the validity of the theories of evolution and natural selection?"

"Not the slightest, let me reassure you—or, do I disappoint you? But at times I do think all of that unwieldy, not very manageable."

"Besides," I said to Sterne, "how can one throw doubt on the evidence of a tautology?"

"What do you mean by that?"

"It seems to me that your criticism of generalities suffers a bit from the same vice as its object. And if one pushes things to the point of caricature, as you did for literature or philosophy, though not without reason, one can say the following about natural selection: Darwinism postulates the survival of the fittest. How does one measure fitness? By survival. Darwinism therefore postulates the survival of the survivors. Is that not a tautology?"

Sterne burst out laughing.

"That suits me perfectly. It is too bad that Lady Savile is not here to hear this delightful blasphemy!"

"Let us go further. The neo-Darwinists, Weismann the first among them, maintain *a priori* that each characteristic of a living organism corresponds to a particular adaptation. Isn't that a philosophical way of putting chance itself under the banner of radical necessity, recalling somewhat the Panglossian reasoning that you flung back at Mr. Richardson?"

"Go on, I beg you."

"Take the absolute and the sacred, which, as you pointed out, account for a certain family relationship between religion, the arts, and philosophy. To them, let us add, with your permission, science, in certain of its manifestations which are scientific only in their phraseology. Many biologists consider the neo-Darwinian theory unalterable, or at least admit its provisional nature only on condition that all subsequent refinements lead in the same direction. Does that not have a smell of mysticism?"

"As a caricaturist, sir, you are easily my equal."

"I propose," intervened Richardson, "that we drink to poetry. Whether it fertilizes the arts, compromises philosophy, or dishonors science, whether it be a manifestation of evolution or divinity, no matter! It indeed appears, listening to you, that it is inescapable, and because of that—pardon my audacity—you seem close and fraternal to me. Let us drink to the dreamer and to the logician, that is to say, to the human mind, and let us now put it into a state of intoxication liable to reconcile it with itself."

"Indeed, only wine can perform that miracle," said Sterne. "So let us drink."

And we drank until we reached that inebriety Richardson desired. Richardson himself passed through alternating phases, during which, exalted, he celebrated the splendors of the world, then suddenly, pensive and tearful, plunged into a kind of lovesick melancholy. Finally, completely drunk, he buried his head in his arms crossed on the table, and began to weep.

"I want her to love me, Henry. I want her to love me . . ."

He continued to chant this touching refrain, lower and lower, and fell asleep.

"You see," said Sterne, "where the cult of beauty and the fascination of the impossible lead a literary temperament, to this heartrending tyranny of feeling. Poor Laurence! Aesthetics can be unkind. He probably doesn't know it, but capable of loving only statues, he enjoys his unhappiness. He takes comfort in the thought that the object of his worship is by definition too highly placed to feel love. Of course he suffers on account of this, but doubtless he would suffer far more if he achieved his aims. Nothing is worse for a lover of the ideal than to attain his goal. It kills the trade. This wearisome poetics of the soul implies, quite aptly, that the physical act means nothing, which is a convenient way to resolve certain contradictions. For Laurence can't be ignorant of the fact that Lady Savile is not, from a physiological point of view at least, a statue for everyone, and in fact, considering the reserve intrinsic to her caste, which covers with a Victorian discretion the very masculine freedom of her temperament and mind, she can on occasion be quite explicit in this regard. It seems to me that she was tonight."

"I beg you, sir," I said, "to stop there. You are falling into that pale psychology you condemned a while ago, and your remarks are becoming embarrassing."

"Well, I can certainly see that Laurence was wrong,

and that drunkenness doesn't reconcile anything. Too bad. In the end, a dash of generality isn't always disagreeable."

He emptied his glass and looked at me thoughtfully.

"You seem to me a double of Lady Savile. My God! Two Jane Sheldons! That's a great deal of honor for an encampment of mere mortals."

"Perhaps it is the effect of the wine on your optic nerve. But if your words are true, the honor is all mine."

We were overcome with laughter, and joyfully dispatched the last bottle. Richardson was still sleeping. Sterne went up to him, put one arm around his legs, the other around his chest, and picked him up with an ease and strength that revealed muscles of steel and an astounding resistance to alcohol.

"It is time to put this child to bed. He is ordinarily sober as a Spartan, as becomes an elegiac poet."

He took his leave and went off in the moonlight. The camp was asleep. Near the door of the enclosure, two watchmen were seated beside a fire of glowing coals that turned to bronze the ebony of their chests and faces. Richardson's tent lit up for a moment, then fell back into darkness. I saw Sterne come out of it and head for his own. He waved to me on the way. He lit a lamp, moved about for a time in its light, then put it out. Our own tents, which Lefèvre, following our hosts' organization, had ordered set up on either side of the central pathway, were dark and quiet. Lady Savile's alone shone in the semi-darkness, with a uniform, dim yellow light, but I no longer detected any movement inside. I remained there, seated at the table, pensive, stirred by tumultuous feelings and struck with languor, attracted and repelled by the poles of this magnetic point from which I could not tear my eyes. Finally, I got up and slowly went towards it. The canvas door was open. I stopped at the threshold and looked inside, both cursing and blessing an inebriation capable of giving me enough audacity or recklessness to commit such an act, which my last reserves of lucidity made me consider infamous. Two kerosene lamps shone on furnishings that were almost comfortable. At the back of the tent, stretched out on a camp bed protected by the transparent veil of a mosquito net, Lady Savile was sleeping, still in the dress she had worn to dinner. Thinking back to the last words she had addressed to me, the pressure of her fingers, and Sterne's remarks which had troubled and irritated me, I considered this open door, these burning lamps, this sleeping woman whose appearance suggested more a defeat in the face of fatigue than a desire for rest. All of this perhaps meant she was waiting. But I did not exclude the hypothesis of an interpretative delirium born in me of a deplorable conceit. In either case, my position was delicate, to say the least, and I could not decide which posture was more contemptible: forcing a woman who was offering herself to wait, or forcing myself on a woman who was not offering herself. No doubt it was better to confront the risk of being taken for an imbecile than the certainty of being taken for a lout. This thought convinced me to flee. I wanted, nonetheless, to feast my eyes on this delicious tableau, and I looked one last time at the bed. I felt all the color leave my face. Lady Savile, as calm as could be, fixed on me her blue gaze. For what seemed an eternity, we observed each other, motionless and silent. Finally, she drew herself up on one elbow and said:

"Close the door, would you?"

As I was not making the slightest movement, she added, with a touch of impatience in her voice:

"Well?"

"Forgive, madam, my confusion, and one final lack of tact, which could not make an already hopeless case any worse, but I do not know which side of this door I am to be on after closing it."

She laughed briefly. Then she lay down again, slid her long dress up over her legs, and began to caress herself slowly and skillfully until she reached orgasm. Not for an instant, not even at the very peak of pleasure and abandon, did she stop staring at me.

Two hours later, I dove into the Sassandra. My clothing lay scattered on the stony slope that formed an indentation in the high riverbank. Breathing the warm air between dives, I rolled my body over and over in the narrow corridor marked out by stakes projecting from the current, which slid among them with a continual wet whisper, thick poles planted in the riverbed from one end of the stockade to the other to prevent an intrusion into the camp by predators from the water.

At last I let myself float on my back, looking up to the heavens, while in the west, at the extreme periphery of my field of vision, the shadows of a far-off thunderstorm ate little by little into the nocturnal brightness of the pure sky. These impressions, recorded mechanically upon my retina, superimposed themselves in my mind on detailed images of a white body, by turns lively and languid, slender and full, and of a face beautiful and calm to the point of abstraction, or animated to the point of ugliness; on an evocation without distance, barely detached from a reality so close that it still refused to transmute itself into pure memory, of gestures and words which, in brief scenes, calculated or impromptu, of perversity and passion, expressed all the nuances of obscenity and followed all the complicated meanderings of desire. Suddenly, I heard a scraping on the other side of the stakes. A monstrous head appeared, trying vainly to get past the barrier. In a blind rage, exasperated at the nearness of a prey it could not reach, the crocodile made the water foam, and its spray fell like rain in the protected area. The pincers of a formidable jaw, slipping sideways into two interstices in the barrier, seized one of the stakes and shook it. I was incapable of the slightest gesture, terrified and fascinated by this brutish fury exploding less than a meter away, in a shadowy light that increased the horror of it. I heard a yell, the sound of a jump into the water, very close, and someone pulled me by the arm. It was one of the watchmen from the Gold Coast. There were two deafening shots, then quiet. On the other side of the stakes, a long shape began to drift downstream. A rifle in his hand, a giant was standing on the bank.

"God forgive me!" said Fielding jovially. "One would think we were at the seaside in Harwich during the bathing season. You, sir, are quite a character. . . ."

The storm's first thunderclap, drowning out his voice, rolled over the jungle, prolonged by an echo that seemed like a dull growl in the throat of an irritated feline. The camp's population was gathering little by little at the edge of the river. I got out of the water, embarrassed to be the cause of this disturbance and to be making such a spectacle of myself. Standing somewhat apart, Lady Savile was observing me. Darkness enveloped us, and the rain began to fall in torrents. In the cold white glow of a bolt of lightning, I saw her again, her soaked dress clinging to her body, her long hair smoothed and plastered down around her head by the water, which brought out the pure oval of her face. And as the lightning continued, all of us watched in its intermittent flashes the successive apparitions of this feminine splendor, immobile in the midst of the outburst, impassive in the multiple and gaping maws of savagery.

"My intention," said Lady Savile, "is to observe, most particularly in the behavior of chimpanzees, the phenomena of aggression and dominance, to verify if the correlation between supremacy in combat and privileged access to resources, food, or females, for example, is valid. I do not know whether this corresponds to your own plans."

"My project, madam, is vaguer. I was intending simply to study their habits and gestures, without structuring my observations, before considering the possibility of drawing any conclusions from a particular type of behavior."

We were alone in her tent, seated on opposite sides of the cluttered table that served as her desk. One might have believed, from the detached tone of our conversation, that our relationship consisted of nothing more than a purely professional exchange. In truth, there was nothing spontaneous about this detachment on my part; rather, I was basing my attitude on hers, persuaded that the expression of an emotion that found no echo was always somewhat ridiculous and importunate, and filled with suspicion, not to say fear, before the risks of displaying feeling. And yet the simple fact of seeing and hearing her moved me to the point of worry. I did not know whether this woman felt for me the indifference that follows a random adventure, or some sympathetic interest and, if the latter, whether her intellectual and emotional behavior were separated to the point of schizophrenia or she had such control of herself that she was able to conceal the slightest trace of the previous night.

"I would also like," she said after a silence that betrayed some hesitation, "to begin to verify a hypothesis I have been thinking about for several years. You are the first person with whom I have decided to discuss it. I resolved to do this without being able to determine clearly if what prompted me was based on our professional relationship and if my reasons were purely scientific."

"Whatever they may be, madam, they touch me. I

pray you not to consider me in any way a competitor."

"I do not know," she said smiling, "if I am capable of such innocence. Here is my hypothesis: according to Darwin's model of evolution and natural selection, organisms can act only in their own self-interest and struggle to increase their offspring, that is to say the representation of their genes, to the detriment of their congeners. No higher principle exists in nature. Personal advantage is the sole criterion of success, general equilibrium comes from a pure interaction of individual egoisms. But the theory runs up against serious obstacles, which, incidentally, did not escape Darwin himself. To begin with, insect societies, where evolution, by creating sterile drones, goes in a radically opposed direction. Also, in a number of species that live in collective societies, altruistic behavior has been observed. Further, if we admit that altruism is the highest moral value and the bond of human society, it would mean, if we were to respect the letter of Darwinian theory, that human society is fundamentally foreign to nature and that the fruits of consciousness are absolutely independent of biology, which I, personally, cannot accept. It would amount to postulating the unique origin, if not the divine essence of our species, in spite of everything we know about evolution. How then can one reconcile altruism and biology, or, in Darwinian terms, altruism and natural selection?"

"I suppose one way would be to question certain aspects of the theory itself."

"That would amount to establishing a new rule based

on the exception, which, you will agree, does not seem reasonable. I have rather sought a solution within the theory, and I have arrived at a mathematical extrapolation of the most recent genetic data. We know that the genes of each individual resemble the genes of its family members to a degree that varies in direct proportion to the closeness of kinship. If for an organism the fundamental principle of nature consists, as Darwinian theory would have it, in augmenting to the maximum the representation of its genes, and resides solely in reproductive success, then there exists a great number of cases where an individual, governed purely by instinct, would find it in its interest to sacrifice itself for its close relatives, if they are sufficiently numerous, because all of them together would have a greater capacity than it alone to propagate its own genes. This is what I would call family selection, or proximal selection, which makes altruism a sophisticated form of egoism, that is, of the law."

I looked at her with undisguised admiration.

"Do you mean that in order to favor its own reproductive success, it is in the interest of an individual to sacrifice itself for a given number of siblings, or a greater number of cousins?"

"Exactly."

"And that would make human morality and biology compatible, insofar as our consciousness would have simply seized upon this instinct to make of it an absolute, positive value, altruism, by extending it to larger units, such as social class, nation, culture, or, more rarely, alas, the entire species and even the whole of all living things."

"I really do not understand why we insist on systematically attributing to the mind what we consider noble in ourselves and to instinct what we consider base. It recalls the foolishness of dualist philosophies which postulate a radical difference of essence between the soul and the body."

"It is a good thing Mr. Richardson was not present for this conversation, which would undoubtedly have had an effect on him."

"It is a good thing," she said a bit dryly, as if my remark had annoyed her, "that Mr. Richardson is unaware of certain things. There are people who cannot confront all realities."

"I am convinced, madam, that you are not among them."

She looked at me fixedly, then turned her eyes away. She soon recovered.

"Let us please stop speculating on the improbable," she said, "whether it be scientific, philosophical, or personal, and whether suggested allusively or not. Instead, tell me what you think of my hypothesis within the more concrete perspective of our work on chimpanzees."

"It is a brilliant theory. Its experimental verification, however, would seem to present serious difficulties. In my view, it would require at least three types of measurements: first, the degree of kinship, possible if the study of a population is sufficiently long and detailed;

second, the costs and benefits of a particular behavior, a measurement practicable only in extreme cases and which must be made—an additional obstacle—independently of real reproductive success. This last point is important, because if one analyzes *a posteriori* an ensemble of behaviors in terms of reproductive success, one risks falling into a tautological trap: if reproductive success is high, then the behaviors which preceded were beneficial, and the inverse, if success is meager, they were costly. There is a serious risk of confusing 'as a result of' with 'in spite of.' The fact that a monkey has a fall and subsequently engenders numerous descendants could lead to the conclusion that the best way to facilitate reproduction is to fall out of a tree. To take up a theme from our conversation of the other evening, there is a bit of Pangloss lurking there. The last measurement is that of reproductive success itself, perhaps possible in a laboratory, but very uncertain in the field. I want to make clear that these difficulties do not discourage me in the least, and even constitute an unanticipated stimulation. I am grateful to you, madam, for your splendid theory."

Her glance at once struck me. It expressed a combination of excitement and something that seemed close to tenderness.

"I would like us to make love," she said. "Now."

The following morning, the first joint expedition left the camp. It consisted of Lady Savile, Sterne, Fielding, Lefèvre, our ten Abidji porters, and myself. The blacks from the Gold Coast remained behind under the supervision of Richardson, who had no scientific or geo-graphical competence, and was a poor bush traveler besides. We continued upstream along the Sassandra to the junction of the Bafing, which we followed straight west on its right bank. Lefèvre and Fielding walked at the head of the group, side by side, the one with his short and precise step, tireless, the other with immense and slow strides, like a peaceful Sunday stroller in Hyde Park. We could hear them talking and laughing. Be-tween this giant and this dwarf there reigned a true *entente cordiale*. I was pleased to see Lefèvre so much at ease, since my prejudice against him had subsided little by little in the wake of our altercation at the Bandama encampment. The two of them were followed by the Abidji, lightly loaded. We had brought along a minimum of equipment, in order to reduce the number of porters and increase our mobility. Behind them Sterne ad-vanced at an easy pace, now and then turning round to Lady Savile and myself, who brought up the rear, to toss out some pertinent and humorous commentaries on the character of our group, a botanical curiosity, or a remarkable feature of the landscape. Jane talked to me about the relative failure of previous expeditions, analyzing it and proposing various strategies for avoid-ing the same mistakes. I answered her as best I could, making a constant effort to follow her conversation, held less by the content of her words than by her way of pronouncing them, the expressive musical inflections of her voice, and also the play of her features, the grace and confidence of her walk, and the harmonious movement of her long legs traveling the rough path with ease. From time to time, she took a white silk scarf, fastened to her wrist and moistened with water from the river, and ran it over her face and down the bare neckline of her man's shirt, which was open to the top of her breasts. She did this more out of pleasure and coquettishness than out of need, since she did not seem to be suffering at all from the heat. She eventually noticed my distraction, and took my hand, laughing. Never, not even in the moments of fiercest pleasure and passion, had I so wanted to tell her that I loved her. She seemed happy, and I wondered whether this stemmed from action, closeness to the experiment, and the hope of discovery, or from an emotional state. There was a certain melancholy in this question.

The middle network of the Bafing vanished upstream into the central depression of the western mountains, which were cut by its course into two chains arranged in a horseshoe around this almond of low and torrid territory, a kind of equatorial greenhouse drowned by rains, where the explosion of vegetation at times became limitless. The Touba massif blocked the northern horizon. Its tabletop buttes resembled truncated pyramids, whose steep sides, often nearly concave and ending in cornices, a profuse flora struggled to climb. In the south, the Man mountains raised up two colossal bastions, the Toura massif, close by, and the Dan massif, receding into the western background, a proliferation of heavy knolls linked by passes and separated by high valleys where streams flowed in overwide beds strewn with blocks of stone and debris torn from the slopes.

In the intervening jungle, the colonies of chimpanzees were abundant. We caught a glimpse of them fleeing at our approach. When night fell, Lady Savile had camp set up in a clearing surrounded on three sides by a bend in the river. I shared a tent with Henry Sterne. Our conversation, lively and animated, lasted far into the night.

One month later, we were reunited in the same place, in a very different mood. Our observations had been difficult and inconclusive. The chimpanzees were wary, and our presence modified their behavior, which falsified all of the data of the experiment. They tended to move about constantly in order to get away from us, and stopped only at a distance where any research became problematical, if not impossible. Lady Savile, upset in the extreme, did not open her mouth except to make some brief remark in a curt tone about problems of organization and of work. Our relationship had gradually changed, and this, on top of our scientific failure, threw me into a permanent state of cold rage. I went so far as to ask myself how I could have such strong feelings for her, all the time knowing that this infantile thought was nothing but a pathetic defense against a racking anguish. Lefèvre had fallen back into his usual taciturn mood, and Sterne's irony was becoming aggressive, as if he were trying to pick a quarrel with the entire universe. Only Fielding retained, in the midst of the disaster, an unshakable sense of humor that sufficed to prevent a general explosion. Aggravating further our state of mind, driving rains, which had made the undergrowth into a veritable cesspool, had followed one upon another almost without interruption.

All five of us were in Lady Savile's tent, while outside torrents swept over the jungle and the foaming river, whose swollen waters were overflowing their bed and threatening to invade the site where our camp was set up.

"We cannot continue this way," said Lady Savile. "Our data are scarce, and lack an indispensable continuity because of the chimpanzees' nervousness. On the other hand, each of us, no doubt to compensate for the dearth of observation, tends to indulge in somewhat hasty personal interpretation, instead of confining himself to more objective and patient description. This gives rise to such contradictions that the whole of the assembled data seems like a nearly unusable tangle. It would be appropriate, at least for the moment, to make use of one's eyes more than of one's imagination. This criticism, sir," she added, turning to me, "does not apply to you. But your extreme prudence, not to say your reserve, leads me to suspect a certain skepticism on your part, as if our methods were discredited in your mind, which hardly helps improve the climate."

"Grant me, madam," I responded dryly, "the paternity of my own methods. And if I find them ineffective, please believe that I hold only myself to blame."

"Perhaps your mind is not entirely on what you are doing?"

"Perhaps, madam. But in that case, what on earth am I thinking about?"

A shadow of sadness passed over her eyes, which made me regret my insolence, even though she had deliberately provoked it.

"It seems to me," said Lefèvre, breaking an uncomfortable silence, "that the major difficulty is the alarm felt by the monkeys. Everyone here, taken individually, behaves in the jungle with tolerable discretion. But as a group we are about as delicate as a herd of elephants, which is hardly conducive for passing unnoticed. We should set up much smaller groups, working at a respectable distance from each other, and not on the same population."

Lady Savile seemed to take note of his existence for the first time.

"That is the only good idea expressed since the beginning of this expedition. I am very grateful to you. Here is what we are going to do. You, sir, will leave, accompanied by Samuel and two porters, for the Man mountains in the south, provided, of course, that does not overly offend your touchy independence," she said to me with a smile. "Mr. Lefèvre and Henry will head for Touba country, in the north, with two porters as well. I shall remain in the Bafing area and will continue to observe the population already studied. We could meet again here, let us say in a month, to take stock of the situation and prepare what follows. Does that suit you?"

"On one condition," said Lefèvre. "That I leave my best man to assist you. He has traveled in the jungle with me for fifteen years, and I have absolute confidence in him. He speaks a little French and will transmit your orders. He is an excellent hunter and an original cook. His recipes for game with slightly toxic mushrooms are famous throughout the lagoon area. They have a euphoric effect. Come to think of it, it would not have been a bad idea to make use of him lately."

"Another thing, madam," interrupted Fielding amid laughter, "I must ask you to beware of leopards. I believe them to be sufficiently discerning gourmets to find aristocratic English flesh tasty, which might prove annoying, even if they act with no real malicious intent. At all times be armed and accompanied by an armed porter who can shoot quickly and accurately."

For the first time in weeks, dinner was pleasant and relaxed. As if to ratify this change in atmosphere, the rain stopped, and we could dine outdoors, around a large fire that whistled and crackled because of the dampness of the wood. The moon, lighting the jungle with a pale glow, climbed into a sky gradually freed of its heavy vapors, a dense bank of which was being pushed towards the east by the night wind. My exchanges with Lady Savile that evening were courteous and measured, as if there remained in our behavior some trace of the masked antagonism of the previous days and of the recent altercation which had been its consequence. In fact, caught in a perverse mesh of willful misunderstanding, I probably exaggerated that impression, by reason of a state of mind that pushed me to interpret Lady Savile's normal discretion as pure and simple coldness toward me. I therefore feigned polite indifference throughout the dinner, while denouncing to myself the ridiculous sentimentality that fostered such an attitude and doing my best to believe that this indifference, which I had always taken to be the dominant trait of my character, was real and not put on. But my circumspection with regard to others and myself is more spontaneous than studied, and when disarmed by an irresistible force, thus unwillingly betrays a certain vulnerability. Because of this, and because of a scientific training oriented towards the search for truth whatever the cost, I have little endurance in dissimulation. I wound up sinking, with a considerable increase in sincerity, into a melancholy which led me to take my leave abruptly.

The next morning, after the departure of Sterne and Lefèvre, Lady Savile accompanied me for a moment, at some distance from Fielding, who, followed by our two porters, was leading the way. We walked along side by side in silence. She stopped. "Your attitude," she said, "makes me think that in this climate things decay more quickly than elsewhere."

"You know perfectly well that is not true, madam. Let us just say that, with regard to the English aristocracy, I find things less simple than do Mr. Fielding's leopards."

She smiled, took my face in her hands, and kissed me. Then she turned around and disappeared in the direction of the camp. As I was catching up with Fielding, I thought back on the mixture in this woman of the spontaneous and the tactical, the effect of which was a power of seduction such as I had never before encountered. Abandon and willingness in pleasure; private passion and public reserve; respect for the letter of propriety and indomitable freedom; keen intelligence, theoretical genius, and philosophical weakness when confronted by failure; the expression of an affective and professional trust in having explained her hypothesis to me, and of distrust in having switched the guides so that there would be an English presence in each expedition; and now, this last gesture, delightful, coming in the midst of irony.

We established our camp at the foot of the Toura massif, two days' march from the Bafing. Fielding turned out to be a charming companion, and with time his conversation revealed, beneath the deliberate mask of humorous pragmatism which in my eyes had till then been his only face, an uncommon subtlety and sensitivity. My research was solitary. At dawn, I went into monkey territory, while Fielding remained a good distance away at the campsite, which we moved whenever that distance became too great. Thus we followed, prudently, the slow travel of the animals and the whims of their itineraries. The guide took care of provisions, and went hunting far in the opposite direction. Day by day I got a few steps closer to the chimpanzees, and the distance I had to maintain so as not to seem an intruder—signaled by a noisy concert of howls and a sudden agitation that made me beat a retreat—imperceptibly diminished. I was still not able to come close enough for easy and efficient observation, but I was beginning to glimpse the way of getting there. It was a question of time, patience, and discretion, precluding any sort of collective investigation. It was, in short, a question of solitude.

When the month had run out, I hesitated to interrupt my progress, fearful that an absence would cause me to lose ground, and I was tempted to draft a first report and entrust it to Fielding. Eager, however, to learn the experiences of the others, and above all see Lady Savile again, I made up my mind to rejoin the encampment on the Bafing. We arrived there two days later to discover with concern that it had been reduced to two tents, in front of which Lefèvre, accompanied by a single Abidji, was waiting.

"We came back here three days ago," he told us, "after a rather fruitless journey. We found Lady Savile bedridden with a high fever, half unconscious. We immediately made a stretcher, and she was transported to the base camp in the care of Mr. Sterne."

We set out again at once, even though the sun had disappeared behind the foliage and the eastern sky had begun to darken. I was so worried that I decided we should cover at a single stretch the distance separating us from the Sassandra, a decision both the guides approved. After twenty hours of walking, during which we accorded ourselves barely four hours of rest, we arrived the next day, at nightfall, within sight of the high stockade of the English camp. We were met by Sterne, his face marked by sleeplessness.

"We made such slow progress," he said, "that we arrived here only a few hours ago. Quinine helped Lady Savile bear the trip, but her fever is now reaching alarming proportions."

We disposed of our equipment and went into the tent. Lady Savile, stretched out on her bed, frightfully pale, her eyes half-closed, bathed in sweat, was shivering all over. Richardson was wiping her forehead with a damp cloth. I looked at her dejectedly for a moment, then I moved forward, took her in my arms, and left the tent. I headed for the Sassandra. I went into the river with my burden, and plunged it into the cool water. The current, encircling her white face, which alone emerged from the water, slid along her cheeks and her temples, making the long, untied locks of her hair ripple downstream. The others had followed me and were watching, silently, planted on the shore like statues of salt. I had a feeling of exalted distress, of a violence unknown to me, which, added to the drug of accumulated fatigue and the tension of my will repulsing with all its forces the idea of death that invaded my mind, exhausted me. Lady Savile at first struggled feebly, then let herself go. Little by little her trembling eased and her features relaxed. The fever had started to drop.

In the middle of the night she awoke and asked for something to drink. Roused from a half-sleep, I lit a lamp and brought her some water. She seemed very weak, but perfectly conscious. The quinine had completed the work begun by the cold bath. In sickness her beauty had taken on a somehow touching quality.

"It seems to me," she said, "that I fell in the water and you took me out."

"No. I threw you in."

"The last resort against the fever?"

"Yes."

"How long have I been in this condition?"

"I don't know. Sterne and Lefèvre found you this way five days ago."

She stared blankly for a moment.

"Everything is rebelling," she murmured. "The body, things, feelings . . ."

"Feelings?"

She fell silent again. She seemed closed and defeated, as if in effect she was discovering with confusion and bitterness the weight of a world over which, for the first time, her intelligence and her will had no power.

"Yes," she said finally, "feelings. The chaos of feelings. The jungles are winning. And not only the jungles of illness and of wild beasts. There is you . . ."

"I, madam?"

She was on the verge of tears. I was going to take her in my arms when she spoke again. Her voice was infinitely tired.

"You make me vulnerable and scattered. Every day you are more and more of a burden on my mind. It comes at the wrong time. I would like to free myself of you, in vain. You are an unwelcome emotion for me, a pleasure that drives me to despair. I believe this amorous distraction is the main cause of my failure, and perhaps of my weakness in the face of illness."

After this strange declaration of love, which made me feel a bit like a dog that has been pelted with marrow bones, I had the choice of either surrendering myself to her definitively or backing off, offended. Desiring the first possibility, I heard myself act on the other, with a cold exasperation resulting less from Lady Savile's words than from my own inability to resist my inclinations, my enslavement to mistrust.

"You slander yourself, madam. I believe your heart and mind too well organized to yield to such a vulgar affection, in all senses of the term. No proximal selection impels you to show any altruism whatsoever on my behalf."

She seemed profoundly shocked by this miserable derision, and looked at me with surprise, then anger.

"Precisely," she said icily. "From now on, we are going to apply ourselves to respecting the law."

"Well, madam, if you permit, I, for one, am going to try to prove it wrong."

I left abruptly. I went to awaken Richardson and asked him to take my place at Lady Savile's bedside. Then I went into my tent and filled a backpack with the following items: writing materials, a map of the area, a compass, a small medical kit, binoculars, two boxes of a hundred 7.65 cartridges, a coil of rope, toilet articles, some clothes, and a hammock. I buckled around my waist a belt from which hung my Walther pistol and a hunting knife. Thus equipped, I entered Lefèvre's tent and woke him up.

"I have decided," I said, "to go observe the chimpanzees alone. I will not come back before obtaining satisfactory results."

"I rather think you will not come back at all. Would it be indiscreet to ask what is pushing you to commit such a folly?"

"It doesn't matter. I will be going rather far, near the Dan massif, in the direction of Mount Nimba. Make sure the English don't come to sightsee in that area and disturb my work. Tell them the first thing that comes to your mind, or the truth, as you like."

"And when should I begin to search for your remains?"

"If I am not back in a year, you can return to Abidjan. Here is a letter releasing you from all responsibility and acknowledging your services, for which I have only praise. Here too is the key for the chest containing the money. You will pay the salaries punctually, every week."

"Seriously, are you really going to do this?"

"Where did you get the idea that this might be an attempt at humor?"

He began to laugh, without aggressiveness, then sighed.

"Being in love," he said, "is without doubt a very beautiful thing, but it is often accompanied, in the most reasonable people, by a certain amount of stupidity. What do you want to prove, and to whom?"

"Stupidity consists in playing at psychology, of knowing the answers even before hearing them."

"If you do not come back, I will go looking for you, and I will find you, dead or alive. I stake my reputation on it."

"As you wish. But not before a year. Do you hear? Not before a year."

"I am not deaf."

"Farewell, Lefèvre."

For the first time, I extended my hand to him, spontaneously. He accepted it, shaking his head. Shortly afterwards, I left the camp under the intrigued eyes of the watchmen, whom I had asked to open the door of the enclosure. Proceeding up the Sassandra, which glimmered under the setting moon, I headed for the junction of the Bafing. The jaws of the jungle closed on me. I was going, my head full of dreams, crushed by solitude, into the heart of darkness.

The high foliage was bathed in the blazing dusk, and the jungle prepared for the terrors of the night. To the southwest, the vertical wall of the Nimba was taking on tinges of dull gold, blood, and shadow, at the will of the changing intensities of the sunset. In the undergrowth, darkened by the uninterrupted plume of great trees, a premature night, as if come from the earth and not the sky, was creeping in. The stilt roots of the niangons and uapacas, garrotted with lianas and sheathed in epiphytes, disappeared into the oblique blackness that was slowly rising to the tops. From a pond came the croaking and wet flight of batrachians threatened by some thin-bodied aquatic snake, a killer enveloped in silence, distinguishable only by the delicate ripples of its swimming, come to trouble the absolute quiet of the still waters. Clusters of flying foxes and epaulet bats detached themselves from branches and scattered about in quest of fruit, stalked in the open spaces of the waterways by the buzzard standing out against the dark blue of the sky, anxious to put to good use the too-brief time of a hunt begun in the final radiance of the vanished sun and destined to end with the coming of darkness. The galagos were awakening as the shadows deepened, saluting the coming night with their strange cry, like the sobbing of a human child. A giant Seba python, asleep or lying in wait, hidden in the folds of its own rings, was motionless as a stone. High up, the chimpanzees were arranging their temporary dormitories. At the top of a nearby tree, I installed myself in my shelter, a kind of vegetal cage whose floor was several large branches crossed to form a crude platform, and whose walls and roof were a latticework of thick poles, cut vines, and supple twigs growing nearby. With pieces of rope I reinforced this structure, which was strong enough to withstand a surprise attack by the leopard, the only predator I had to fear since I always chose trees with smooth wide trunks and no low branches, thus discouraging the great python and sparing myself the proximity of smaller and more dangerous species, mortally venomous, that proliferated on the ground and in the lower vegetation. I had acquired a certain dexterity at this task, and could now build such a shelter in less than an hour. In its center, my hammock was stretched in a fork, and my knapsack, stowed on a branch, hung at arm's length. Lying down, I remained awake, listening to the murmurs of a savagery amplified by the progress of the shadows, and watching the flight of the darkness over the jungle with an emotion and a dull fear that habit had never succeeded in lessening.

Ten months had gone by since my abrupt departure from the camp on the Sassandra. I had been able to rejoin, not without difficulties, the chimpanzee population chosen during my expedition with Fielding. It consisted of nearly thirty subjects, which made it rather easy to spot, since the other chimpanzee societies I had encountered on my way seldom exceeded ten. During my absence it had moved off to the west, a migration through a vast territory that had led it, always in the ombrophilic forest of the central depression, from the Toura to the Dan massif, in the direction of the Nimba. It had taken me five months to achieve a satisfactory proximity to the monkeys without causing panic or an aggressive reaction. I had gradually become a familiar part of their universe. Although I had thought it possible to make myself completely accepted by them through the practice of mutual grooming and delousing, very important to this species but something I had not considered without a certain repugnance, I had decided to seek proximity rather than adoption. Thus I had not overstepped a limit of thirty meters for fear that a more direct sharing of their life, the effects of which I would not have been able to evaluate with precision, might modify their behavior without my knowing it. This distance, nonetheless, allowed me extreme ease of observation. In the following five months, I had collected a considerable amount of data, which were now beginning to show some signs of organization.

The absolute novelty of this existence had meant for me a complete initiation into the jungle and into solitude, an apprenticeship which, imperceptibly, had turned into reflexes that spared my mind a permanent mobilization for survival and allowed me to devote myself to study. I had learned to spot safe shelters and consolidate them with the means at hand. My diet, copied from that of the monkeys, consisted above all of fruit, which was abundant year round. While compared to the chimpanzees and other even more agile species I seemed extraordinarily clumsy and heavy, I had acquired a certain sureness and a respectable competence in the incessant climbs made necessary by my search for shelter and observation posts and my need to reach the trees' fructiferous zones, which, owing to the absence of light in the undergrowth, were frequently elevated. I made use often of the rope I had brought. I had become, then, a tree dweller and a fruit eater. I ate meat very rarely, forbidding myself, so as not to frighten the monkeys, the use of my pistol for hunting and even defense, except in a case of absolute necessity, of mortal danger, which had not yet arisen. On occasion I would kill small rodents with a stick or with my knife. Then, reluctant to consume the game raw, I would move away from the chimpanzees' territory to build a fire. Because of the loss of time caused by these carnivorous episodes and the scant dietary benefit and pleasure I derived from them, I had finally resolved to abandon hunting altogether and give myself over exclusively to gathering.

The most difficult and distressing part of my integration into a world where aggression and murder were banality itself, the elementary, daily law of equilibrium, had been to cultivate a perpetual mistrust, a constant alertness of the senses, which gradually substituted itself for the calculations of an intelligence too slow and sluggish to command effective reactions. I had had to learn to detect without delay—that is to say without thinking, something made possible by a kind of permanent suspicion—animals that were dangerous for me, and this in an environment where their very survival was a strict function of their discretion, their ability to pass unnoticed. I had also had to learn to foresee their reactions and to tightly control my own. Curiously, the greatest danger came not from animals that I considered hypothetical predators but, on the contrary, from those in whom I caused fear, and therefore, in certain cases, a defense reflex. The first, the predators, were the leopard and the great Seba python. The leopard, until now, had kept its distance, made wary by my size, appearance, and odor, all foreign to its experience. This monkey-killer, who could find more familiar game in abundance, doubtless did not care to run uselessly the risk of the unknown. The python was slow, except in a very close-range attack, and almost never reached sufficient size to consider me an easy prey. The second, the most dangerous, were poisonous snakes. I had distinguished four species, which had become for me the stealthy image of death: two terrestrial, the black cobra and the knocking viper; one species both terrestrial and aquatic, the six-horned viper, whose skin was decorated with shimmering colors and refined geometric designs; and one arboreal, the green mamba, whose terrible bite, unequaled speed among reptiles, and perfect homochromy rendered it particularly fearsome. I could not be a prey or a competitor to them, but only a vague danger. They therefore never attacked me deliberately, and preferred flight to self-defense. Even in this last case, they gave some visible or audible warning designed to avoid a confrontation by forcing me to remain beyond the point that would make striking an absolute instinctual imperative: a swelling of the hood, neck, or entire body; a threatening movement of the head, vibrating like a tight spring; a sudden burst of designs and colors turning in an instant from camouflage to its opposite, a dissuasive signal. My initiation had consisted in learning to avoid this moment of imminent death, a moment which had presented itself several times early on, when only a rapid and horrified retreat had saved my life. Now, during the travels forced on me by the incessant migrations of the chimpanzees, I almost automatically examined the folds in the bare ground; likewise I scrutinized with care the middle vegetation before attempting a climb, and the low greenery when I found myself at the edge of areas where a gap in the ferns, allowing the sun to pass through, permitted plants and grasses to cover the earth. I carefully scouted ponds before drinking from them. I proceeded slowly, making a measured noise, too faint to frighten the monkeys, loud enough to warn of my approach any long mamba lurking on a branch, any viper coiled in a hollow on the ground. In the thickest and darkest places I used a light, thin pole, the end of which sometimes suffered the whiplike attack of a killer disarmed by the impassive hardness of the intruder. Progressively, my fear wore off, permitting me to satisfy a curiosity about reptiles which I had felt since childhood, and on occasion I observed the calm and terrible hunt of a snake that I had spotted from far enough away so that it was not concerned with me. The fascination with horror and disgust, so common among my fellow men before a creature they had made the cold and crawling symbol of absolute evil, corresponded in me to a fascination with strangeness which was not exclusively scientific and was mixed with I don't know what kind of obscure sympathy.

I had nothing to fear from the other species haunting the jungle, which put me into a position of security nearly equal to that of the leopard, the undisputed master of these savage realms. Nonetheless, I was the perpetual witness to unlimited murder, which oppressed me with a vague and tenacious anxiety. In every animate form I saw a condemned being, on the look-out, desperate, in the exaltation and joy of existing, to postpone indefinitely the final suffering, to prolong a reprieve always on the eve of expiration. I dreaded ceaselessly the murderous gravity of daily existence, the cruel games of hunting and escape, a rule of life which in my mind still had that exceptional quality which cold and limitless violence holds for our species. In the twilight reddening over the western horizon, I discovered, with a fascination and a terror that never faded, a sort of glorious reflection of the blood spilled beneath the peaceful cloak of branches which covered with their green folds attack and flight, cries of triumph and fear, desperate leaps of denial and convulsions of agony. In this chaos, by a perverse harmony of balance and efficiency, there was a mysterious beauty that was almost always associated with violence. It suffused the savage ballet of predators and victims pushed by instinct to a perfection of movement, and contaminated even death itself, a death furtive and muffled by silence, or full of noise and fury, death according to the serpent or according to the leopard.

And then there was the sweetness of the mornings. The first hours of dawn inspired a kind of truce, an interlude between the nocturnal predation and the hunts of the day. The foliage, washed by the night's downpours, was greener and more brilliant, adding to its overflowing and unordered vitality the savage discoveries of natural composition suddenly made perceptible by some secret effect of lighting. I would leave my vegetal refuge and slide down the rope to the foot of the giant that had sheltered my troubled sleep. The chimpanzees moved about in their high dormitories and unhurriedly began their first gathering of fruit, stopping to observe me while I washed and shaved in the water of some pond where the aquatic snakes, disturbed, moved off nonchalantly without trying to strike. In the topmost plumes of the trees, splendid and multicolored flowers blossomed in the dawn sun, whose oblique rays, penetrating the gaps in the foliage, gave the jungle below the muted magnificence, the glorious peace, of an extraordinary cathedral.

At the mercy of the effects on my mind of this permanence of opposites, serenity and violence, order and chaos, beauty and horror, pairs superimposed on an absolute solitude which took on in turn the masks of drunken freedom, desperate oppression, or delicious melancholy, my vision of things altered, caught between the caprices of sentiment and the bare rigors of reason. At times this world forced itself on me with a strength and clarity that put me into a state near happiness. Its serene and terrible course demanded none of those weighty, complicated, often inept justifications that consciousness believes it necessary to invent in order to find itself tolerable, impelled by its irrepressible demand for finality. Murder seemed to me integrated into a vast and irreproachable harmony, subjected to the strict law of survival, which controlled it by keeping it from any useless act, any gratuitous cruelty. I saw in this economy, compared to the excesses of my fellow men, the expression of an innate wisdom, a form of tolerance. The splendor of the jungles contrasted with the hideousness of the cities, the competence and adaptability of wild

organisms with the baleful incompleteness and awk-
wardness of civilized species ever in quest of a tool to
prolong life or perfect death. I felt myself filled with
the power and the clarity of this natural world, linked
organically with the totality of a universe that had no
other justification to offer than its existence alone, and
in which the loss of any part was but an episode, quickly
healed. I rejected with elation and contempt the useless
and cumbersome baggage of metaphysical or moral
speculation, hollow rhetoric inspired by fear, being
myself in these moments free of all dread, seeing in
death, ever on the prowl, a simple transformation of
matter. At times, on the other hand, I felt full of terror
and indignation at the brutality of the aggression, at
the pangs of anguish and physical suffering around me.
I began to hate this world, occupied solely with destroy-
ing itself better to endure, with regenerating itself by a
continual baptism of blood. The whole blind and fero-
cious mechanism seemed to me an absurdity. The per-
petuation of unthinking, purposeless matter did not
justify suffering, and I wished only to return to my
fellow men, to their capacity for intelligence and kind-
ness, the memory of which inspired in me a limitless
nostalgia.

These extreme states, quite rare, were only the critical
moments of an excess of solitude. Ordinarily, I did not
deviate too far from that blend of curiosity, calculation,
stoicism, and humor that should make an indispensable
philosophical base for any man of science more or less
worthy of the name. What had changed in me in a

durable way, more in the emotional than the intellectual realm, was my feeling of vulnerability in the face of a universe where words no longer had weight. I had always lived in an environment ruled by the power of words alone, and I had spent my life making of them as much a means of defense, a carefully constructed wall between others and my own sensitivity (reduced thus to the silence of a voluntary *in pace*), as an instrument of investigation and knowledge. But here, now, this wall had lost all effectiveness, and in order to endure, that is to avoid flight, madness, or death, what was necessary more than physical strength or force of character was one's own absolute truth. The jungle, then, was completing the ruin of this wall already shaken by Lady Savile, the irresistible seduction of her mind and her flesh, and the passion she had caused to be born in me, a passion painfully restrained by a shameful marvel of circumspection, a frantic rejection, set down as an absolute principle, of any possibility of suffering. Besides the contrary ravings of exaltation and indignation, I was filled with melancholy, woven from the jungles of the real and the affective, from Jane's body and the savage matter of things, from solitude and truth. I was as if naked in the dawn of a world.

These moods found an echo even in my scientific activity, the interpretation of the data of my research. I gave a good part of my time to the chimpanzees, but, being in a situation where a considerable number of varied phenomena continually solicited my attention as a naturalist and biologist, I did not stop there, and tried to study the totality of the environment, the jungle in general. I have already stated my interest in snakes. On several occasions I had had the opportunity to observe the two great predators of monkeys, the leopard and the crowned eagle. I had also thought it useful to proceed with a comparative examination of the habits of other primate species within the perspective of the theory formulated by Jane, particularly with regard to dominance and intraspecific rivalries, and I regularly spied on groups of cercopithecus, mangabeys, and colobins. As I had foreseen, I managed more or less to establish the degree of kinship, which required long and difficult observation; but it was impossible for me to measure the costs and benefits of all the monkeys' behaviors or real reproductive success. Nonetheless, the prime importance of kinship imposed itself on me, and certain behaviors plunged me into confusion, born of contradictory hypotheses concerning the universal genetic imperative and individual reactions, egoism and altruism, general selection and proximal selection. Nothing allowed me to prove Jane's theory, but neither did anything invalidate it absolutely. This made me appreciate once more the gulf separating the behavioral sciences from the exact ones. These contradictions led me to formulate a criticism of what seemed to me the greatest danger of neo-Darwinism and its totalitarian spirit. Just as, in my view, all the characteristics of an organism did not necessarily correspond to a narrow and utilitarian principle of adaptation, so experience tended to show me that an organism was not the simple support, the slave of its own genes, subject only to their will to propagate themselves. Rather, it represented an inseparable entity with, according to the degree of its evolution, its perplexities and even, ultimately, its choices. I saw in this a kind of hesitation in instinct, and even more in learning, something decisive among the chimpanzees, for whom the competence necessary for survival seemed to depend more on the acquired than the innate. I even came to ask myself whether the complexity of behavior, that is to say, the manifestation in certain individuals or species of conduct apparently aberrant with regard to the general law of selection, so ingeniously re-evaluated by Jane, was not a function of the importance of learning as compared with instinct. I thus forged, obviously without being able to prove that it was real, a chain between nature and culture, animality and humanity, whose links connected instinct to learning, learning to innovation, innovation to consciousness, consciousness to morality. I came back, by an indirect route, to what Jane had said to me about intelligence and instinct. But while she, thanks to her theoretical genius, was able to reason within the bounds of orthodoxy, I could not be totally convinced by the simple perfection of a system which too many facts seemed to resist. The law had to be appreciably more complex and, no doubt, plural.

Curiously, it was an event which seemed to verify Jane's hypothesis satisfactorily that determined the end of my research. The monkeys almost always exhibited a social sense that manifested itself in the relative benignity of the dominant ones towards the other members of the group, notably in what concerned access to females and various resources. This was also apparent in the case of danger, but in a less obvious way, and I had never observed any extreme altruistic behavior, in my opinion for two reasons: the leopard and the crowned eagle struck isolated individuals, and their attacks were of such lightning speed that in general the alert came too late. On such occasions the dominant males were content simply to issue a warning, while themselves taking shelter, and their angry cries accompanied the assailant in its retreat to a place where it could devour its prey in complete tranquillity. The eagle almost never assaulted chimpanzees, except for young ones straying incautiously away from the group, a very rare occurrence, but preyed on smaller species, particularly mangabeys, who frequently came down to the ground. Its attack, its manner of killing by crushing the head of the victim in one of its claws with such force that sometimes the brain was expelled from the cranial cavity and the eyes popped out of their sockets, its retreat—all of this was instantaneous, and before its prey could make the slightest gesture or its companions sound the alarm, the hunt was over. The leopard was slower, and it sometimes missed its target. One day, I was observing a group of females and young on the ground, vaguely watched over by a dominant male to whom they were related and whose strength, extraordinary agility, and prudence had, until then, served primarily for self-protection. Suddenly a leopard leapt from the undergrowth. The male saw it at once, jumped up howling, which I took for the start of an escape, then landed back in the same place, pushing away the other monkeys who quickly reached the upper regions. It lasted a second, but in this gesture I saw a conflict of incredible violence between proximal solidarity and a frantic desire of the organism to escape death. For the male it was too late. It just avoided the first contact with the feline and began to flee in my direction. When it smelled the musky breath immediately behind it, it did an about-face, a derisory counterattack that had something deeply moving about it. In an instant, the monkey was crushed. This all took place a few meters from me. The leopard, after making its kill, looked at me, and no doubt seeing in me another predator liable to rob the fruit of its hunt, came forward growling. Being on the ground in a very vulnerable position, I had, from the beginning of the attack, taken my pistol from its holster. I raised it and emptied the magazine. The animal turned back on itself, screaming, came down in convulsions, and, its eyes open, its head fouled with blood, froze beside its victim in the immobility of death. Rarely had I experienced so violent a series of emotions. I let myself sink down next to the feline and buried my face in its fur. Overcome with trembling, I felt my tears flow. And I did not know whether I was crying for the monkey, the leopard, or myself, my love, my fear, and my solitude, controlled so long and now in a crisis overflowing. Perhaps, out of anguish and pity, I was crying simply for the world.

The chimpanzees, who usually remained noisy and agitated for some time after an attack, were invisible, immobile and silent. In this there was no doubt an unprecedented reaction to an event completely outside their experience, a state of terrified stupor, caused by the gunfire and the death of an invulnerable enemy, obliterating an ordinary fear, a learned rage in the face of the banal murder of one of their own. From then on, it was impossible for me to approach them again, and they fled from me as if I were the leopard itself. I decided, with a mixture of relief and regret, to put an end to my research, and to return to the camp on the Sassandra. I had stayed for ten months in the jungle, which sometimes seemed like a second mother to me, a savage initiator who had made me discover concretely the brutal truth of things.

I set out one morning for the network of the Bafing as the sun, emerging through the foliage, lit up the eastern wall of the Nimba. And it seemed to me, leaving this place, that I carried away with me, within me, forever, a trace of violence and solitude, the stamp of a permanent melancholy.

I arrived at the camp one evening. I stopped some distance away, full of a sudden apprehension at the idea of renewing contact with my own kind, and, above all, of seeing again a woman whose image, embellished profusely by the wanderings of an imagination inflamed by distance, had progressively taken on the dimensions of a myth. Behind the high stockade, reflecting the final glare of the sunset, wreaths of smoke rose straight up in the still air and vanished into the deep blue background of a cloudless sky, which darkened toward the east with the approach of night. A nonchalant watchman was leaning on the frame of the opening, and running a distracted glance over the thick edges of the nearby jungle. From time to time a call or laugh could be heard. This peaceful murmur, this ordinary noise of a human society, filled me with gratitude and nostalgia. I stood there, savoring the pleasure of the delay, soaking up the familiarity of things.

Finally I set out. As I advanced I felt the weight of an ever-heavier anguish. Old emotions assaulted me, and I sensed a kind of involuntary stiffening of my thoughts and attitude. I had to admit that I was afraid. The idea of seeing Jane again filled me with dread. Irresistibly, without premeditation or control, I was rebuilding a defensive wall against her and against myself. The lookout, alerted, watched me approach. We recognized each other in the same instant. It was the man who had jumped into the Sassandra to save me from the attack of a crocodile. He came forward, touched me, began to laugh, then saluted me and turned around, shouting. I stopped him, and went through the opening of the enclosure. I was now inside the camp.

With mounting anxiety I headed down the central pathway toward the "dining room." They were all there, around the table. They had heard the watchman's cry, and stood up at my approach. I stopped several steps away. We looked at each other in silence. Sterne and Fielding smiled at me warmly. Lefèvre's face expressed an emotion that I had never seen in him before. In Richardson's gaze there was a mixture of perplexity and sympathy. Jane stood before me, very pale, more beautiful than all the reconstructions of memory enlivened by dreams, more beautiful than all the figures of desire and passion that had obsessed my solitude. I took out of my pack an enormous bundle of ink-blackened papers, and held it out to the young woman, at last making up my mind to speak. I did not recognize my own voice, hoarse, broken, and low, with something mechanical about it.

"Here, madam, are the results of my observations. They contain no scientific proof of the validity of your theory, but more than enough to support its formulation as a hypothesis. All of this is a bit premature, considering the inertia of our minds, the weakness of our means, and the uncertainty of our methods. You will be admired, envied, but not followed."

She took a step towards me. Her lips were trembling.

"Why have you done this?"

Doubt was still pushing me to evade a question directed at the obvious, a question that asked, not for a rational answer but for an affirmation of feeling.

"If I told you that it was out of pure scientific concern, would you believe me?"

"No."

"Then there remain only a few possible answers. What can I tell you that you do not already know?"

"Say it!"

Suddenly I returned to that simple obligation to truth which had come to me in the jungle. The wall of circumspection, rebuilt for an instant, collapsed again. For the first time, I accepted being without defenses.

"Because I love you."

Saying these words to this woman, in these circumstances, filled me with unimaginable happiness. She came to me, put her arms around my waist and, burying her head in the hollow of my shoulder, she wept for a long time.

I n the scorching night the ship advanced toward the east, plowing through the thick black water churned up by its propellers, which drew on it a whitish line, an open and bubbling wound that remained in the distant sea like a scar of foaming eddies. This wake seemed extended to the maritime horizon by the flickering reflection of the moon setting in the western ocean. The ship was proceeding with powerful slowness, its engines throttled, indifferent to the languid swell that slid beneath its enormous hull to vanish and die, a mile to the north, in the inextricable jungle of the mangrove swamp. Leaning on the guardrail of the upper deck, I observed the lazy stirrings of the sea, the irregular outline of the African coast receding to port, the passage of heavy banks of vapors against the luminous backdrop of the nocturnal sky. Beneath me, soldiers slept right on the deck, or sat up, talking in low voices and smoking, producing a vague murmur punctuated now and then by a cough or a laugh. A petty officer walked up and down nonchalantly, his hands crossed behind his back. I heard, without seeking to make out their meaning, snatches of a conversation between Sterne, Fielding, and Lefèvre. A little farther away, seated on a canvas folding chair, Richardson seemed lost in a morose reverie. Reality, though it persisted, sometimes became diaphanous. The powerful images of a recent past superimposed themselves on the decor of the present and disturbed its contours, creating bizarre frescoes which jumbled the worlds within and without, made of perception and of memory, in which my story contracted to the point of incomprehensibility. The sea and the night had the transience of a dream. Against a background of water and sky studded with light there passed before my eyes, obsessively, a cascade of forms whose increasing speed gradually took on the character of a free fall. The common thread in this fleeting chaos was Jane, every feature of her face, each detail of her body, all the poses of her nakedness, the nuances of her expressions, the tonalities of her gaze. In this example of an encyclopedia confined to one single flesh and limitless in its refinement, there even emerged the image of the images of her I had painted with the colors of solitude. Then, all at once, things fell into place, with their weight of logic and nostalgia.

It began with the jungle. Then my return to the camp and her spontaneous gesture of love, at last, which had marked forever my mind and my memory. The trip down the river to the port of Sassandra, full of gaiety and perils, of passion and accidents, a time of an intensity and a violent joy such as I had never felt until then, a sort of late dawning of an ideal adventure of love and childhood. I was happy to the point of bliss, audacious to the point of stupidity, without defenses and invulnerable, and on this subject I made speeches to Jane of an irony that made her burst out laughing. Then the trip by sea to Grand Bassam aboard a coaster, the arrival at the port, the crossing of the lagoon, and the meeting, in Abidjan, with a governor more bewildered than ever in the face of a situation whose scale and brutality overwhelmed his simple sense of duty: war had just broken out in Europe. War! Our dejection before this immense and sordid news. Blanchot had instructions for us. Jane was to return to England as soon as possible. The men were mobilized on the spot. Sterne, Fielding, and Richardson had orders to return to the Gold Coast and to put themselves at the disposal of Lieutenant Colonel Bryant. Lefèvre and myself, at the head of a platoon of district guardsmen, were going to join Commandant Maroix's troops in the Pobé region of Dahomey. The mission of the allied forces was to besiege German Togo and take over the radio installations at Kamina, a transmitting station in direct contact with Berlin. The following night, we were to take an improvised transport, a commandeered merchant vessel heading for Cape Coast and Cotonou. Jane would remain behind. She was to await a steamship leaving Grand Bassam two days later for Europe.

Dream and disorder returned at the end of this cold chain of events, which, in a few hours, had made of us, who had tasted the powerful freedom of a world where our only duty was to understand, simple playthings of circumstance, wisps of straw to History, which was crushing all individual choice in its arbitrary mechanisms, its massive machinery of laws, hierarchies, and interests. Dusk bathed the veranda. The setting sun slid through the shutters into the bedroom, drawing horizontal lines of light and shadow on the bed and Jane's naked body. A body animated by the boldness of desire, distorted by pleasure, then exhausted, plunged into a torpor in which I could not help reading, already, some sign of a necessary oblivion. A striped body which now possessed me, offering itself tirelessly. And then my departure, or my flight, in the night, the crossing of the lagoon, the lights of the port and of the great ship, the vibrations of the engine, dull beats of a colossal heart that were like the amplified echo of my own, the very rhythm of separation, the exact measure of the irreversible. Finally, the vanishing into the west of the last glow of a world about to topple, the consummation of a break at once private and universal, and our lumbering progress into the emptiness of the open sea.

I suddenly came back to reality, and the conversation taking place behind me, which Richardson had now joined, reached me clearly.

"For a specialist in animal behavior," Sterne was saying, "this war will no doubt be interesting to observe. A kind of apotheosis of intraspecific rivalry."

"I doubt there will be anything there to joke about," interrupted Richardson.

"My dear Laurence, I am perfectly willing to admit that my duty lies in making my modest contribution to this raving madness. But even so, you cannot ask me to do it seriously. I do not have sufficient moral conviction to rebel or to break into patriotic songs."

He turned to me and continued:

"You must admit this constitutes an unexpected follow-up to our collaboration. I am delighted. It will be a pleasure to be hacked to pieces in your company, that is if you do not again decide to go it alone, which, let it be said, would in this case be the most reasonable course to take."

This remark struck me. Not for a second had the idea of deserting crossed my mind. Since attaining the age of reason I had always believed myself above simple collective values, different from the multitude who blindly hand the reins of their destiny over to others more competent than themselves, capable in all circumstances of exercising my free will, more or less persuaded that the fact of observing the world with the distance and detachment of a scientist placed me, by a sort of contamination, in an analogous position with regard to common ideology and morality. But this was only a crude illusion, a pure and simple boast. I was not different from the millions of men who, since the first great concentrations of the human species, had killed or been killed without profit, without hate, without understanding, automatically, in a way that excluded even the most elementary perplexity. I was myself perplexed—not that that gave me any advantage over them—and conscious of a question to which I could bring no answer other than this: I was fulfilling an absurd duty, participating in an enterprise about whose undertaking I had not been consulted, in the name of an ethic whose murderous absurdity I felt deeply. I came back to the jungle and to Jane's hypothesis. I thought of the chimpanzee killed by the leopard, crushed by the apparently contradictory, no doubt secretly coherent dictates of an instinct which, playing against itself, had triumphed over a frantic desire to live. At least one could suppose that the monkey dimly knew, because of the narrow limits of its universe, why or for whom it was dying. Perhaps duty managed to convince so many people to lose everything for an unknown reason because it conformed to an instinct long buried beneath the rhetoric of moral discourse, but quite alive. Perhaps the absurdity came only from the great numbers and the anonymity, from the fact that those whom one killed and those for whom one was supposed to die fused together in the same ignorance. And the tragedy of this ignorance rejoined the tragic immensity of the killing.

Jungles

A young man came up and leaned on the guardrail next to me. It was the lieutenant whose acquaintance I had made on the crossing from Europe to Africa. Still impeccable, fresh and rosy, he graced me with his childlike smile. After the usual greetings, as I made no effort to start a conversation, he remained silent for a time, brimming with good intentions he was eager to express somehow. Suddenly he said to me:

"Did you end up finding your sea crocodile? You remember, the one that was so out of place?"

I looked at him amicably and wearily.

"Not in the flesh, Lieutenant. But I believe I have made some progress in understanding its mentality."

I looked again at the sea. And I thought I could see, in the wake of the ship, the plunging of a monster on some endless voyage without destination, solitary in the midst of a limitless unknown, fleeing the narrowness of the shores and their laws, forever a stranger.